THE MIRROR

RON LAMPI

LAMP LIGHT PRESS
(831) 251-0225
thelamp66@gmail.com

The Phases

Prologue

A devotee of Aphrodite one day gave Ral a mirror. Judith was a friend he had known for some years, since the time, in fact, when he had first arrived in Santa Cruz. She explained to him when they talked on this auspicious day that she was once again going to have to move and couldn't take the mirror with her. *Here, you can have it as a gift*, she said. *You're a Goddess poet, and I think you're the one who should have it.*

It was a perfectly round, large Moon mirror (as Ral came to call it), plain to its edge, no frills, having a plywood backing, with an extended wood bracket screwed into it for mounting. It took two hands to pick it up and carry it. *So, you can look at yourself in all your vanity*, she joked. *Maybe you will see something. Maybe Aphrodite will speak to you.*

Ral gladly received it and was open to what she said. Yes, he could see himself gazing into it and meditating in it, and just maybe he would see something more to himself, or maybe even something other than himself.

And so Ral carefully carried the mirror out to his car and put it in the trunk and drove up to his modest abode on the mountain, some miles from the town of Aptos. He took it out, brought it inside, and nestled it in a cushioned chair, against its back. This was when Ral lived alone on the mountain, before Rhonda moved in. In the evenings, in another chair facing the mirror, he began a practice of gazing into it, in a stilled mind, slowly developed, meditative trance. The mirror was so like a full, round, reflective Moon. He didn't know a thing about the art of mirror scrying, but he naively grew into his own practice. And how indulgently self-conscious it felt in those early days. But soon after, he began hearing this voice, the voice of the one he knew—Psyche:

You will study yourself in this mirror.
You will pierce through the narcissistic gaze.
You will go into the mirror and learn many things about yourself.
You will go into it to where you do not recognize yourself.
You will not know who you are, who this is staring back at you.
You will puzzle yourself. Perhaps you will feel alarmed.
You will unmask yourself and see all the different guises of Self.
You will discover another, Higher Self…

So Ral would gaze into the mirror…
And Psyche came to him again,

You will find another Mirror.
Your life will not be the same.

Ral was puzzled by that. And years went by without him really remembering this…

Finding The Mirror

It was the year 2012.
To find a way into oneself, one should simultaneously
find a way into a Greater Reality.

One afternoon in sunny May Ral was exploring somewhat off the beaten track in a nearby forest up in Felton—The Santa Cruz Mountains were all thickly covered by forests, one could even get lost in places. As he slowly walked, the forest, the air, were eerily quiet. He felt that. He continued to walk on soft redwood ground, and as he was casually walking, unexpectedly, surprisingly, he came upon a small, stilled pool of water such as he had never seen before. It was a pool so still that all the surrounding trees were perfectly reflected in it. But more than that, it was a pool almost unreal how round it was, and it had a presence of such tranquilly in all the forest around it. It didn't have anything floating or growing in it. He was immediately curious about finding such a pool, so he stepped up closer to it, and stopped to look into it. He could easily see his reflection, but as he peered a moment longer more intently—it was crystal clear—he realized he could see through the water's mirrored surface. Then he saw something shining through the surface, appearing not that far down, as the pool was not deep at all. What he saw was shiny and appeared also to be perfectly round. He could probably reach down for it, if he wanted to. So, he thought, why not? He then rolled up his sleeve and reached his hand on the impulse that followed into the water and touched what was a smooth, hard surface. He felt around to the edge of it and grabbed it and so brought it up out of the water. He found that it was a round mirror, relatively small, oh, about the size of both of his hands, his fingers outstretched and almost touching. It had a thin metal band around it with suddenly moving symbols. *What?* The symbols now appeared to brighten, as if subtly illuminated. *What is this?* He was quite startled. He knew them as the astrological symbols of the zodiac. Oh, yes, and there were planetary symbols interspersed among them. *What? What's going on here? How is this possible?* Then, *How did this mirror get into this pool? Who put it there? Did someone purposely drop it in and left it? And the pool?*

Ral immediately sensed, though, that there was something even more unusual about this mirror. When he looked into it more directly now—as obviously anyone would think to look into it—it was as if he was magnetically drawn further into it…he was riveted. And it was certainly strange what he was beginning to see happening in it now: He saw these shifting, inchoate forms; amorphous, shifting forms moving about in it. These forms, in variegated colors, began to sharpen, they came into sudden focus. Ral was shocked. Suddenly he saw in the mirror living, shifting pictures of the world… It opened deep into pictures of places and landscapes—he saw meadows, fields, farms, towns. He saw rivers and waterways, ocean cliffs…remarkably he looked out over the enormity of ocean… And then rolling hills, mountains, forests, and deserts he saw… And then streets of houses, cities he saw, towering cities, and the wide boulevards of cities, and of course people flashed in it, especially streams of people on the streets and sidewalks of the cities… More thoughts flashed across his mind, *What's happening here? I can't believe this! This is simply amazing…it's unreal. How is this even possible? How is this happening? Am I hallucinating?* He was now in an altered state.

As he stood there, absorbed in the passing pictures of the mirror, he now noticed that a face was beginning to appear as if superimposed over the change of scenes. Quickly he saw that the face was his face, and as his image became more pronounced, the scenes faded away, until all he saw was now his own reflection. But then, in the next moment, something more started happening—his reflection appeared to sink back into the mirror into a further 3D depth. His reflection sank further back into the mirror, and now a space, as if his face had dissolved, opened. This space expanded deep inside the mirror, and he saw numerous tiny mirrors appearing in it, as if floating in it, slowly dancing around. He now saw himself in tiny images that reflected back-and-forth in dozens of ways among the mirrors. There now appeared to be corridors of mirrors spreading out in all directions. And he could look down into the corridors until they disappeared in the distance. He realized that all these mirrors were simultaneously reflections of, and windows into, his own soul…because he realized that these were familiar places in his soul, in his psyche, but the magic was that he could now visibly see them. He was witnessing the various aspects, the dynamics, of his psyche in action. At the same time were bursts of insight coming at his witness of a pure "I" about every big and little thing in his psyche. His I, his Ego, his familiar self-image of an Ego, appeared to have been disassembled: various complexes he saw…his shadow, his critic, his self-conscious alienation, and various subpersonalities; he saw the palpable energies of his hurts, his worries and fears, his anguish, his shortcomings and weaknesses and frustrations…his presumptions, his judgements…and he also saw his joys and yearnings and the things he loved. Yes, he saw his partner, Rhonda. And each moment of accompanying insight made impact, an impact that transformed them into self-understanding, but an understanding that further transformed them into immediately effective changes where changes that he had needed were called for. These were all not only realizations about himself personally, but further in the distance of the corridors were hints about himself in a larger space of all human psyche. And far in the distance of corridors that were just dark, but like a watery dark, he seemed to hear a cry…yes, it was coming from deep inside this other dimension that had opened that had this distant, echoing sound—*a cry*… It was a plea even. He felt overwhelmed, as if blasted, to be witnessing all of this, yet some transformative process had been triggered in him and would be irreversibly underway. He felt that his Ego had splintered into a thousand pieces and was then reconstructed by scintillations of Light. His Ego had this moment become a clear pool, simply reflecting. He realized his heart was beating faster, and that his life suddenly felt unreal.

He turned his eyes from the mirror; he had to look around—yes, the forest was still there. He was back in his senses, but at the same time he still felt altered, in an unreal state. He had to wonder, *What just happened? I can't believe this. This isn't the reality I know. And would it happen again? Could it?* He looked into the mirror again. And yes, shapes began forming in the mirror. He realized the process he had experienced was beginning to happen again…

Ral had to stop, he glanced away; he paused a moment longer, rather shaken. He slowly gained more clarity. What a precious find was this, he then obviously had to think. This was—paranormal magic, was it not? What a gift, to have found it! Was it meant for him to find it? It was too much to even try to comprehend what had happened. He realized that he hadn't looked at the back of the mirror yet, so he turned it around. He saw on it a beautifully exquisite complexity of circles, spirals, curves, and lines, and letter-like glyphs that were— ciphers of some kind? It had a soft, faintly golden, matte surface. It looked like it could have been a work of abstract art. This was obviously all the work of an Intelligence—the whole mirror obviously was the work of an Intelligence. But he was not in a state to speculate about it further; for now, he felt himself in a surreal state that wasn't about to be analyzed. And he felt an unexpected joy.

He knew that he had to take this mirror with him back home. Was it just him? Would it create the same experience for others? He immediately thought of Rhonda, his partner; yes, she would confirm if indeed the mirror could produce the same experience in her. The thought came to him: *I need to share this, but I need to get myself out of the way too.*

Ral retraced his steps out of the forest, clasping the mirror tightly as he carefully walked. He found his way to his car and put the mirror on the back seat, being very careful not to look into it, and covering it with a shirt. The mirror he realized had a magnetic draw that he had to resist. He had to sit for a few minutes. Though still a bit spacey feeling, he started up his car and drove—he didn't have to drive all that far—, keeping his focus, thinking that his life would probably be changed forever. And thinking all the while, *How was this experience in the mirror even possible?*

All the way home, Ral also kept thinking, *Is it only me?* He was then soon at their house; he would quickly show the mirror to Rhonda. He came in the front door with the mirror still wrapped in a shirt; she was in the kitchen that was all part of one open space of kitchen, dining, and living room that the front door opened to. (He was renting the house with money (along with others) distributed from a deceased great uncle who had millions. At this time, he didn't need to work.) To Rhonda, he appeared to be in some sort of altered state. Did something happen? Or was it that some remarkable news had occurred?

You look really agitated or something, she said, stepping from around the counter.

He was quick to reply, *You won't believe this. Here, I want to show you something that I found that is simply amazing…simply marvelous. More than that, way more than that. It is rather unbelievable.*

Rhonda looked puzzled, even concerned. *Really? Well, what are you going to show me?*

So Ral went on, *I was walking in the woods up by the quarry earlier and found a pool of water like I've never seen before— I looked into it and pulled out—* But then he stopped, it was too much to explain; all he wanted to really say was, *Look what I found.*

Yes? she looked at him quizzically, while also seeing that he had something hidden in a shirt. The way he said all that made her very curious. *And what is it you got there?*

Here, let's go into the living room and sit down. I will show it to you and hopefully you can see for yourself. You will not believe this. That's if it happens for you. Otherwise…

She still didn't know what to make of what he was saying. They went into the living room and sat on a two-person couch.

Here, all you'll need to do is to look into it, said Ral.

Look into it? What am I looking into?

And so Ral removed the shirt from the mirror, and ever so slightly turned its mirroring side, but not directly, towards her; he cautioned her not to look directly into the mirror, not yet. He didn't show her any of the backside. Rhonda said, *Oh, a mirror, so?* and was puzzled a moment by it. She now immediately saw, though, something of a band that looked like astrological symbols encircling it; she also knew astrology. So where did he get it? And why did he turn it to the side, not directly at her? But a certain aura she now felt coming on. Again, he said he found it up by the quarry in the woods in a perfectly round pool. He saw something shiny in it and pulled it out of the water. It was this mirror he was now holding. *But how did it get there?* she asked. He had no idea. He then turned it around so that she could see the backside. *What kind of alien script is this?* she asked, in puzzlement. He obviously couldn't say. She gazed at it for a few moments. So far nothing made sense…but she felt something. Something was pulling on her.

Okay, are you ready for an experience? he asked. *I hope you have an experience like I did.* He now turned the mirror side around again.

An experience? she said, again rather puzzled, but feeling something. Was it not just a mirror? And yet, it did have those astrological symbols, and the back of it was a complete puzzle. And it had this presence about it; she was now sensing more of that already.

Yes, just look into it now and see what happens. Ral was obviously hoping that she would have an experience like he had. He didn't want to be the only one. Was he going crazy? He now turned the mirror so that she could look directly into it.

Why was he really emphasizing that she look into it? Look into a mirror? What's so special about that? But she was still sensing something more; she now gazed into it. He held it for her while she gazed. And she was indeed irresistibly drawn into it.

Rhonda sat there, staring into it, and was transfixed. She quickly became lost in it. She saw amorphous forms become 3D changing pictures of the world, just as Ral had seen. She saw her face appear and then open into a deeper space. She saw a curious dance of mirrors, and then corridors of mirrors. She was seeing, she realized, the various inner dynamics of her own psyche. Certain conflicted energies that she had in her psyche suddenly shifted. Secret concerns, worries, her criticisms, came to life in these corridors of mirrors. Her Ego felt splintered and was reassembling on some other level. She experienced a wave of transformation. She felt, rather uncommon for her, a remarkable joy; her face brightened in a radiance. The worries and concerns that she had nagging her on the periphery of her consciousness were gone. Did she ever need to be critical as before? She then turned from the mirror; some minutes had gone by. That was enough. She had to collect herself, slightly shaking her head. She pondered. More minutes went by as Ral quietly waited.

They now looked at one another. Rhonda shared with him what she saw. And what she experienced closely paralleled what Ral had experienced; he didn't need her complete details; he intuitively knew what she experienced. Ral and Rhonda then hugged each other, kissed, and both said, *I love you.* Their relationship from now on would be fully consciously interconnected, harmoniously interconnected.

Ral now mentioned a few more details of where he had found it, but it still simply didn't sound believable. *A pool, up by the quarry?* Rhonda echoed. But this experience she just had was equally unbelievable, and yet, she indeed did have it, did she not? But…was this—suddenly her thought—was this something occult, or what? But, then, how could this sudden revealing of the inner workings of her psyche be something to be suspicious of? It was rather, in fact, enlightening; she again felt an uplifting joy that issues she had were somehow magically resolved. What immediately seemed to happen between them was a subtle shift of understanding each other, a shift such that they now knew from inside each other what each other would react to, and this new understanding would also make the occasional occurrences of kneejerk, critical reactions suddenly unnecessary. It was particularly this: Of course, they always understood each other on a familiar level; of course, they cared for one another; but the little, trivial, unthinking comments or reactions that simply shot from the mouth that would trigger pointless spats or irksome moments they now could immediately see, and they sensed they would stop. They were suddenly beyond it. Again, they sensed that they could see each other from inside each other. As for the complete experience each had with the mirror, they could not exactly communicate it, but for the sharing of the images that happened to occur in the experience. A profound shift of self-understanding, and of mutual understanding of each other, had occurred.

I feel like I've just raced through years of therapy within seconds, Rhonda said. And then, *How did it get into that pool? And what about the pool?* They went back and forth about this, but, of course, there was no definitive answer. Except for this: Some other Intelligence had to be involved.

Ral wouldn't gaze into the mirror again for that day. Rhonda said likewise. What they both experienced was enough to process for now.

It then obviously occurred to them that they couldn't keep this a secret to themselves. It was first of all contrary to their social dispositions—they circulated widely among various friends, acquaintances, and groups; they also hosted a monthly discussion group. Of course they were going to share the mirror. And the message they got in the mirror itself seemed to insist on them sharing it with others. Both of them that early evening had an impulse to get on the phone with someone; but they held off for now, for at least that evening. Both of them had to reflect on this more. And it occurred to them that they shouldn't lose sight of the mirror. At the least, they had to cover it. Would they have to hide it? Ral said that he would keep it close by during the night; it would sit on top of his clothes bureau, covered. (They had separate rooms.) Certainly, they felt they had to protect it.

When Rhonda saw how Ral was so focused on the mirror, though, she said, *Now don't obsess about it so much already. Let's see how this goes.* But she herself was quietly obsessed about it. Ral could now psychically see that.

Little could they realize just then how the mirror would now direct their lives. And little could they know what more the mirror would reveal. It was time that they had dinner...

The First Days

The next day when Ral woke up after a fitful night when images of the mirror came and went in subconscious semi-sleep, he immediately again, in wide awake consciousness, thought of the mirror. He had placed it the night before on top of his chest of drawers, covered by a black cloth. He got out of bed and looked on top of the bureau to uncover it, just to make sure it was still there, that it was not a figment of a night's wild dream. Yes, it was still there, but he was careful too, as he remembered, not to directly look into it, not yet, not until he was ready to do so.

When Rhonda came into his room (their rooms were on an upper floor), she said again, *Now are you obsessing about the mirror already?* But she said that in a most loving way. From now on their relationship would always be harmonious. Minor differences would easily be handled. They now knew their psyches intimately. They would share a love on a whole new level. They held off for now looking into the mirror. They wanted to prepare themselves.

That morning, they wondered what friend they might first share the mirror with. They wanted first, of course, to share the mirror with a friend, perhaps a few of their friends. They especially wanted to make sure that the experience they had the day before was indeed real… real, that is, for at least one or more others, so that their assumption that the mirror could work its magic for others was indeed correct. What if no one else could experience what they experienced? What then? Was it just meant for them? They decided to invite one friend over first. A friend, perhaps, who had a sense of paranormal matters, who would appreciate hearing, to begin with, what they experienced, even if he or she couldn't also experience what they did. But who would it be?

They now thought of looking into the mirror again. Sitting close together on their couch, they could both look into it at the same time. But something new was showing up in it. Yes, they were experiencing the world and the depths of their psyche, as before, but now some other Greater Reality was simultaneously opening to them. They were seeing images beyond Earth, into outer space, other stars, thousands of times appearing closer, millions of stars, the Milky Way galaxy in a snapshot swirl. Ral was now saying he saw other dimensions opening, yet it was unclear what exactly was opening. Some time went by; they totally lost track of time. But then, that was enough…enough for now. They had to collect themselves, putting hands upon hands, staring into each other's eyes. They acknowledged each other. They kissed. The question again soon came up, Who to call? They didn't know yet, but after breakfast they decided to go into town, into normal reality. They hid the mirror covered in Ral's room, on top of his bureau. They wouldn't share what they experienced with anyone in town… not yet. They spent the day in Felton—the café, lunch, some grocery shopping…all the while holding their breath…not letting on.

It was just by chance, in the early evening, that Henry, a friend of theirs from the East Bay, called. He said he would be down in Santa Cruz tomorrow for a job or two. He drove all over the Bay Area, as far south as Santa Cruz, fixing people's old gas stoves; not many were doing this kind of repair anymore, so he had a constant schedule of clients. He called Ral and Rhonda, as he sometimes did when he was down in their area, to see if they would like a brief visit before he headed back up to the East Bay. Ral took the call with Rhonda standing close by; he said, *Sure, yes indeed, come on over.* They both realized that Henry would be perfect for that first friend they needed. What he did for a living had no bearing really on what his real interests were. Henry said that he would be over tomorrow, late afternoon.

The next day, after hiding the mirror this time in Ral's closet, they went into town again, got their coffees at the White Raven café, hung out a while, then lunch; they didn't want to say anything yet to anyone. They hiked a bit in nearby Henry Cowell Redwoods State Park, renowned for its towering redwood grove. They then did some shopping. Again, the whole day it was as if they were holding their breath.

They had to be back home in time for Henry. They checked on the mirror; it was still there. They sat together reflecting. And soon came a knock on the door—Henry arrived. After a few minutes of casual words exchanged—he already got the idea from Ral over the phone that they had something quite special to share with him—, they had him sitting down in the living room. After they abruptly curtailed the greeting talk, Henry quickly got it that they wanted to get to what Ral hinted was a more serious matter, a more special matter. The energy of Ral and Rhonda was obviously heightening about something. *Wait till you see this*, said Rhonda.

Oh, see what? So what's up?

Henry, look, you almost won't believe what we've experienced if we were just to come out and tell you, said Ral. *You know quite a bit about the paranormal. But this is far more than what we usually hear about it. We want to see if you can experience what we experienced for yourself.*

So, what is this? You're keeping me waiting? What, you got something that special to show me? he said to both of them.

His curiosity was obviously piqued, and for some reason, the thought of psychedelic mushrooms crossed his mind, but he knew that they didn't indulge in that way, and it wouldn't make sense to suddenly just bring it up like this, and besides, it was the way they worded that—especially mentioning more than what usually is considered paranormal—that it had to be something else.

Here, we have something to show you, said Ral. *We're not going to say anything first. We just want to know if you can experience it for yourself. We want you to confirm something. We trust you can handle it, if it happens for you.* Rhonda then emphasized what Ral just said.

Henry was now definitely puzzled. *Take a deep breath, Henry,* said Rhonda, in her straightforward manner. *Prepare yourself,* said Ral.

Henry was so puzzled and intrigued by now. *Let's wait for Rhonda to get something*, Ral said. *Wait for Rhonda?* Henry questioned. He kept wanting to know what's up. So they waited till Rhonda went upstairs to Ral's room to get the mirror, covered now with a flowered silk cloth.

Back downstairs Rhonda held the mirror still in its silk cloth. *What do you have there?* Henry asked. The silk cloth was pulled off, but Rhonda was careful to keep the mirror from Henry's direct gaze. He was now sensing something.

I see that's an interesting mirror you got there. Look at those symbols. Looks astrological. So, it's an astrology mirror. So, what's really special about it? What, I'm supposed to look into it?

Ral and Ronna looked at each other for a second with a secret knowing, at the same time this heightened sense of something they all felt.

Henry, yes, all you need to do is to just look into it, that's all, said Ral. Rhonda handed the mirror to Ral and he held the mirror in front of Henry as Rhonda now watched. They both stood in front of him.

So Henry looked into—was drawn into—the mirror while the two focused on him. His eyes suddenly got big, as he began seeing pictures in it, and was then quickly drawn into its depths…into his own depths, his own labyrinthine psyche depths. He was gone, into the various spaces of his own soul, his own psyche. He was riveted, completely lost in the mirror. And then the Milky Way galaxy opened for him. Ral and Rhonda had stood there, waiting for some ten minutes.

Okay, Henry, time to return, said Rhonda.

Henry was gasping but slowly gathered himself. They gave him a few minutes.

Well, gosh, that's true psycho magic, better than psychedelics. It's—

Yes, so you experienced it. What did you see? asked Ral. Rhonda obviously also wanted to know.

I saw this moving slide show pictures of the world…all kinds of places around the world…and then I saw myself as if I was broken up… the mirror kind'a opened into some depth…lots of mirrors…corridors of mirrors… You know, I saw so much about myself…issues that I've had seemed suddenly resolved…feels like I've suddenly advanced to some level… You know, I seem to suddenly understand myself better. And what, our galaxy I saw? You know, this is like what I heard they call mirror gazing… or it's also called scrying. But this is way off the charts.

Now Ral said that he didn't know anything about mirror scrying… oh, vaguely he had heard about it at some point, as he said he heard about scrying in connection with crystal gazing, like an old friend of theirs was practiced in…

Henry then said, *You mean to say, you know nothing about mirror scrying? It's been around a long time, as far as I know. I say you've just discovered it on your own. But what you've got here is…this is way more of magic than what little I heard about scrying. And a black mirror is used. I don't know anything further about it, really, to be honest, just that it's been around. This mirror has real magic. You have to be careful though. But the vibe I just got is so positive…I'm blown away…it's almost unbelievable, and yet I just experienced it…*

Henry was still taken aback, but he finally asked, *Where did you find this?*

Ral explained as he had explained to Rhonda. Henry said, *So, it had to be some other, what? Some other alien planting of it? In a pool? Here, let me look into it again. I wanna confirm I just experienced what I'm sure I experienced.*

So, they let him gaze into it again. Some minutes went by. He was again taken aback. He stopped, gathered himself for a minute, and then confirmed what he had seen the first time. The message that he got, he said, was that the blast of realization he received was like a first stage…that perhaps another time, the mirror would reveal more. Ral and Ronna concurred that that seemed indeed to be the message they got. And Henry said, still trying to make sense of it all, *This is absolutely a magic mirror. This is another reality.*

And that inspired Ral to say, *I will call it from now on The Mirror, capital T, capital M.*

This is like living psychological astrology then, Henry said. Both Rhonda and Ral agreed.

They now let Henry look at the back of the mirror. He looked it over, entranced.

Wow, that is like some highly involved alien script…a pictograph for what? For doing what?

Henry, we had to think the same, Rhonda said. *It does look like some ET glyph.*

And you found this where? Henry had to ask again.

When Ral again told him, he said, *No, this doesn't sound like the reality I know…*

So the three of them talked seriously about The Mirror for a while. They started exploring the potential implications of it. They agreed that life seemed to suddenly take on a dimension of unreal. When people talked about their paranormal experiences, it was somewhat close to what they experienced, only, whereas such experiences were limited in what was revealed, they saw in this Mirror a tangible, a concrete, doorway to another dimension—Ral said a psyche dimension. And they could hold it, right in their hands, and experience it for probably as long as they wanted.

What if they shared The Mirror with others? The three of them felt that that seemed to be the message. With other friends, yes. *But maybe some researcher?* Henry suggested. Who? What kind of researcher? Ral and Rhonda both said that would be later…it was too soon still to get a big-name researcher involved. It could have its own complications if the story got out in the wider public too soon…and, what if this was a fluke? They needed to keep this local, at least for now. So, the three of them thought about other friends.

Henry promised that he would keep quiet about it, for now, but it would be a little difficult, he admitted. He circulated among so many fringe groups up in the Bay Area; he knew he could easily start talking about it among certain individuals. But, then, would anyone really believe him? What psychedelic was he on? What mere story would he just be rumoring about?

As Henry wanted to do, they already knew the temptation to want to look into The Mirror again. But Henry realized he had to focus himself for the long drive back to the East Bay. So, they let him sit and wait till he was ready.

* * *

Ral and Rhonda had talked about having a small gathering, as soon as it was possible to contact perhaps four of their friends and schedule a day. They often had gatherings at their house—in fact, they held a monthly discussion group there—, but this little gathering for now was going to be enough. This one would be relatively short notice, with a strong hint that they had something rather special to share with the others—this something special was the whole reason for it. They called Henry and he said he wanted to be there again, to be one of the four.

So four of their friends—Erin and Henry, Paula and John—said that they were able to make it and so came over to their house that day. It was a late Saturday afternoon in pleasant, sunny spring, late May. Ral and Rhonda had some snacks and drinks set out for them as usual, so they all indulged while they engaged in some everyday conversation. They all wandered around a bit too, talking in the gorgeous day of the small backyard. But that something special was about to be shared kept hovering among them at the same time. Henry, of course, already knew and was asked not to say anything yet. The question was, What was this mysterious something that Ral and Rhonda kept hinting about that they had to share with them? Some big announcement, or what? They only hinted, hinted that Ral had found something, an artifact you might say, with special properties—they didn't want to go so far as to say magical properties—that they were about to share with them. They said that Henry, who the three others knew, had already experienced it, and confirmed that, yes, indeed, it was certainly out of this world...unreal.

Come on, this is getting to be like some drama, said John. *It's like waiting for the second shoe to drop.*

They had now come back into the house. Ral and Ronna finally had them all sit around in the living room. Ral began, *Okay, are we ready?*

They all looked ready, already primed with anticipation. But they still had no idea what was coming.

If we were to tell you what we've experienced, you probably wouldn't believe us.

Like, Ral, what are you trying to say here? asked John.

What are we trying to say here? responded Rhonda.

Yes, as we've been saying, said Ral, *we do have something extraordinary to share with you. And as we've said, Henry happens to have already experienced it.* The other three seemed more mystified.

Rhonda said, *Here, I'll go get it.* She went upstairs and walked into the hallway into her room this time and came back holding something wrapped in the same flowered silk cloth. The three friends were still wondering with such puzzled looks on their faces what this was all about. This time Rhonda said that she would hold it; Ral then reached over and uncovered The Mirror. Their friends could now immediately see it was a mirror…and so? What was so special about it? They could see, though, it did have what looked like a band around it with astrological symbols. What? The three of them looked somewhat skeptical, like, what exactly did Ral and Rhonda have in mind? What did they want them to do? Just look at it, or rather, just look into it? Rhonda had been holding The Mirror slightly askew. *Why aren't you showing us the full front of The Mirror?* John asked. *You have to be ready,* both Rhonda and Ral said. There was now a heightened energy in the room. Everyone started to feel it.

Now, no need to be alarmed, just relax, said Ral. *Yes, relax,* Rhonda echoed. Then, *All we want you to do is to look into it. We assume—we hope—you will discover something.* Henry himself would hold back.

Again, quizzical looks went around, like, what could a mirror do that they didn't already know, even if, as they saw, it had astrological symbols around its rim? Ral and Rhonda debated for a moment whether their friends would take turns gazing into it but then said that the anticipation for the others waiting would be too much. The three friends were quite puzzled about all of this. So Ral and Rhonda wondered if it were possible for all of them to gaze into it at the same time. Henry already said he didn't need to. A few words were spoken about it really being too small for even the three of them together to look into it directly. Already now the heightened sense they all felt was coming on stronger. But as their friends had gotten closer, huddling together, making an effort to look into The Mirror together, another amazing thing happened that hadn't happened before—what was just a moment ago a two handheld-sized mirror increased slightly in size so that Rhonda had to suddenly grasp it with both hands extended, while she faced it now toward them. And all of them, even Ral, seemed to jump and were all taken aback by this; but this uncanny, surreal, presence had suddenly settled upon them, so that the next moment, they didn't even question this total anomaly. And now all four of their friends—Ral standing back—were drawn into The

Mirror as if it were a magnet, and silently gazed. They gazed for some minutes; they almost didn't want to stop gazing. Ral and Ronna waited and watched their faces. Then, each one, as though they acted on cue, pulled away from The Mirror. Three of them were gasping. Henry, of course, already did that before.

There was silence for a few moments. The three were still taken aback. They all didn't even think to question that The Mirror had slightly increased in size.

Wow, John finally said.

You can say that again, said Henry.

And I'll say simply amazing, said Paula. *That it could open me deep into my inner psyche like that.*

So where did you get this? asked John, with some emphasis. *You don't get something like this in some gift shop.*

Wait, he'll tell you in a moment, Rhonda interjected.

Then, *This is magic*, said Paula. *Isn't this what they call magic? Real magic?*

How does it do that? John, again, exclaimed.

I have no idea, said Ral. *It is a Mirror with paranormal powers.*

Erin, a psychotherapist, who first held back, now said, *It is like an equivalent alchemical passageway into our psyche.*

Ral, Rhonda, and the others, thought that over. And then a *Yes* came out of Ral.

And how did The Mirror enlarge itself like that? John now asked. Of course, Ral had no idea.

Then, *Can we look into it again?* three of them chimed up. Henry himself felt this was enough for now. *Okay, a second round*, Rhonda said. And so, three of them all gazed into The Mirror again for some minutes. Another world—other worlds—now appeared to them. They didn't necessarily all have exactly the same experience though, which Ral and Rhonda would come to realize with others. They then turned away to again collect themselves.

Yes, they did see, again with personal variations, what Ral and Rhonda and Henry had seen. And as with the four, each of them received transformative insights that were personal to them. All made breakthroughs into their own inner dramas, even Erin, an experienced psychotherapist. The amazement was that none of this was felt with alarm; on the contrary, feelings were those of joyful release and relief, for indeed, inner tensions had been transcended. Certain fears, anxieties, worries, just simply dissolved. And more than that, they all saw—better to say, they were beginning to see concretely—how they were all interconnected. And they all still felt—Ral and Rhonda included—that they were in another reality. This had to be something alien…some Other Intelligence was behind it, they all said.

When Ral now told them how he had found The Mirror—he wanted to keep quiet about it until now—, they all seemed to simply accept it, just as they had to accept what they had only moments ago firsthand experienced. But then John asked, *Have you gone back to the pool?* Ral said he hadn't, The Mirror was enough. Yes, it was hardly believable to hear this account of his, but then, no more unreal than the experience they just had. Strangely, it was all now making a sort of sense, especially for Erin, with her own background in Jungian psychology and symbols, which Ral also had.

It seems awfully like how a fantasy story would begin, she said. She looked at Ral, *Are you going to write about it?*

Well, in time, Ral responded.

Then she said, *You know, this has great potential. Think about what this Mirror could do.* Each, from their own perspective, had to agree.

Rhonda, and then Ral, assured them that they would have the same experience again, at another time, if they needed it for confirmation.

…and you would be brought to the same place, Ral said.

So they all accepted that, and all sat back…or kept on the edge of their chairs.

So is there anything on the back? asked Paula.

Oh, we haven't shown you that yet. Wait till you see this— said Rhonda.

Rhonda turned The Mirror around and gave them all a chance to look at it.

Yes, looks like some alien script, said John.

Yes, doesn't it, Erin said.

That's what I thought, Henry agreeing.

Which means what? asked Paula.

So they went on to talk more about The Mirror:

Erin spoke up: *This is far more than what I heard about mirror scrying. You know, scrying has always been a private affair. But this— As you see, this is an immediate jumpstart on self-understanding, that's what. Probably available to everyone. Ral, you do astrology…this must be something you can exactly relate to.*

Yes, it's like astrology in another dimension, said Ral. Rhonda agreed.

Do you realize what this could mean if you got it out to enough people? Erin asked. *Do you realize what this Mirror might be able to do?*

Wow, John exclaimed, *the impact this Mirror could have. As Erin said, Imagine getting it out to other people, lots of people.*

You can say that again, said Henry.

Yes, but how? Paula added.

Yes, how do you get it out to enough people? John too asked. *We all must realize, it can transform people…for the good. It needs to be shared with as many people as possible. But with a plan.*

Rhonda interjected, *But, we gotta start local. Give this time.*

So, you're not going to keep this a secret now? Erin addressed both Ral and Rhonda. They already said they wouldn't.

But Ral had to confirm, *No, not at all. This is why you're here… we're making a start. Look, we are not going to keep this to ourselves. I know each of you would want to share something about this with someone, right? And so, what is the message everyone is getting here?* Ral now asked. *Erin and John already said it.*

Yes, this needs to be shared, Henry said. *But, you gotta realize, there could be trouble.*

You know, it's a sign. It is 2012, after all, Paula then said.

Why yes, why of course, 2012, Mayan prophecy, Ral suddenly realized.

Perhaps humanity is about to make a quantum leap, said John.

Definitely something will happen, said Rhonda. *We can't hold this back.*

They all kept saying among themselves, *Imagine the impact. Imagine if you share this with enough people.*

And Erin had to say again to Ral, *You're a poet. Don't you think you'll be writing something about this?*

And Ral said, *Yes, but I'm still processing. How to even start.*

Their friends had to focus themselves so as to be able to return to the "real world."

Before it was time for their friends to go, they all stood up and formed a circle, with arms around each other's shoulders. They expressed their feelings of connectedness in this experience they all now had shared, and their belief in what The Mirror could do, the good that it could do, that they would hold the intention that this miracle would be used for the good of all. This was a destined breakthrough day… in a time of breakthrough.

What Next?

When their friends left that early evening, each one had to think that some profound launching had taken place. A magic Mirror—and wasn't it a genuine magic Mirror?—supremely paranormal, for sure—for inner work, for inner transformation…for eventual…for what, eventual enlightenment? On some level, at least. *At what level?* And what other world was opening for them? And not to keep it as a secret—as they all agreed, it had to be shared. And it had to be shared freely. And since the question had briefly come up in their discussion, this was not something that Ral and Rhonda said they would think of making money from. Would they charge people for the opportunity of gazing into The Mirror? And each one of them there that day would want, of course, to peer into The Mirror again, to see where it might take them next.

Ral gave something else some thought—he realized that this was not something he would just start blabbing about on Facebook…no, this had to wait. This had to seriously wait. But wait till when? Maybe for some time. How to even frame such a find, such an Experience, such a phenomenon, for posting? He had no big following on Facebook anyway; it was not as if many would even notice what he was sharing, no matter how outrageous it might have sounded. So, there was no point in posting about it just yet. Rhonda felt likewise.

Yes, Ral and Rhonda were still talking this over…they could have kept The Mirror a secret, maybe for a while, if that were possible. But now, sharing The Mirror with a few friends made the possibility of it remaining a complete secret just a little more difficult. And then, could they, would they, hold *their* friends to keeping it a secret? There was no guarantee, even if there was any thought of asking their friends—and any of their other friends who they would be sharing The Mirror with—to refrain from talking about it, that they would all remain completely quiet about it. No, they already said with their friends this needs to go out to more people. But what if they all did remain quiet? What, they would think to have their own little secret inner circle, keeping this genuine miracle to themselves? The message in The Mirror said *No*. They all felt that same intention—The Mirror was to be shared with others.

The four friends they had over that afternoon, even if they were to talk about it with someone—and all four of them curiously enough, were not so inclined, or had any great need, to do so, at least not yet— were also not ones to insist, even if they did mention it to someone, that others had to believe them.

* * *

Ral and Rhonda didn't share The Mirror with anyone else after that, until the Thursday of the month came up when their discussion group would meet at their house. (The group had gone back quite a number of years, back to 2002 at the former Borders Bookstore in Los Gatos, and since that was a public venue, it was more of an open-to-the-public group back then; now that the group was meeting, for the last year, at their house in Felton, it became a more "private" group, still open though to newcomers attending, but more by word of mouth.) Henry, Erin, Paula, and John were all regulars in the group at this time. When the announcement went out via email about the discussion topic (which Ral sent out every month beforehand), they, of course, already had the insiders knowing about The Mirror, which would undoubtedly be shared with the rest of the group. But there was no explicit mention of it, but for the most veiled hint, in the announcement itself. What Ral wrote up (with Rhonda always having her say in this too) and sent out was this:

June's topic: What will it take?
We are going to pose a question to ourselves:
What will it take for our society to move in a
new direction? What will it take for people to
wake up out of their materialistic, consumer
obsessed daydreams? What will it take for
anything of spiritual significance to sink into
the Postmodern mind? Would it be a catastrophe?
Does it have to be a catastrophe? What kind?
On what scale would it have to be? Would it be
an End Times scenario? Totally beyond politics?
Might it be a crippling energy crisis? A radical
global warming scenario? Might it be undeniable,
open ET contact? Might it be the new spirituality
of the New Age dispensation taking hold in
greater numbers of people? A New Age Vision?
So, give this some thought, What will it take?
And we plan to have a surprise in store for the
group related to this topic.

* * *

There were nine participants, besides Ral and Rhonda, in the group this month. Four of them, Henry, Erin, Paula, and John, had already experienced The Mirror, but they didn't say anything to the others, as Ral and Ronna asked that they not say anything quite yet. But hints that something special was going to happen later in the evening kept coming up during their usual potluck before the discussion, and then during the discussion itself. Eric was the only one who really questioned what the surprise in store was that the announcement write-up had mentioned (seemed that most of the time over the years the group's participants didn't always read the whole write-up, to begin with), but, then, of course, four of them already knew what the implication was. Both Ral and Rhonda had to say to Eric, *It's coming.* The discussion theme itself was something that Ral was quite passionate about; it was hard for him to keep to himself about what he saw as the needed New Age spiritual revolution, to begin with…and now, even more so, especially more so, that The Mirror had entered their lives.

The discussion was already a bit different than almost all of them, especially years ago in the public space of Borders, but even for those here at the house. Most of them indulged in wine, as well as the potluck, that had become a part of their house group meetings, leading to a lot of bouncing around of ideas, opinions—politics always about to sidetrack the actual discussion theme—, so much abstract talk, irrelevant tangents, that Ral had always to rein in the potential for a free-for-all—but, at the same time, good ideas, good insights, relevant information, were always shared. Overall, however, the discussions never seemed to go anywhere, never seemed to result in any group action, though all the participants they had had over the years always enjoyed this once a month of getting together. But for this discussion something seemed a little different. There was a heightening in the air.

There came a moment late in the discussion—Ral looking over at Rhonda—when Ral said, *Okay, we're going to have to bring this to a close. Remember, we hinted that we have something special to share with the group, though we've kept it secret that four of you have already had this Experience.* Eyes looked around; so, who already knew what he was talking about? The four of them now let the rest of them know. Ral and Rhonda had to briefly explain that they had had a little gathering of them a couple weeks earlier. So, then, what did the others miss out on, but were about to Experience? Rhonda went down the hallway into a different room and came back with The Mirror, covered as usual.

Ral said, *This, I believe, is what it will take for true cultural change. You are about to have The Mirror Experience.* What? the five of them thought.

Rhonda uncovered The Mirror. The five—Eric, Robin, Lawrence, Linda, Robert—who hadn't experienced The Mirror, again, like the others did when they first saw it, looked puzzled to see it. A mirror? But already a certain increased aura they all felt had permeated the room, once The Mirror was uncovered. It had retained its slightly enlarged size. Again, a brief explanation was shared about The Mirror. The five looked very puzzled. The other four would sit back. This time, Ral held The Mirror.

Wait, this is going to get good, said Henry.

So, the five obliged, looking puzzled, but feeling something, and gathered in close to The Mirror.

Look at those astrological symbols, Eric said. He was also an astrologer. But before any other comments were made, the five were already being drawn into The Mirror. And it, again, slightly increased in size a little more; they could all gaze into it at once. *What was that?* five of them gasped. This itself was amazing and baffling to them. But, then, they all were being drawn magnetically into The Mirror as the others had…

Over some minutes they had their Experience. *Wow!* And *Wow!* again. They were left baffled, but at the same time feeling this wave of good energy. Still, they almost couldn't believe what they had just experienced. A few minutes went by for them to process. And then, so many words were exchanged among all:

Paula first said, *So you all had the Experience, like the four of us had.*

Well, are you back in the real world? Henry had to ask.

Welcome to the new world, was John's reply. Erin herself would listen to the others.

I never in my life imagined that something like this was possible, said Lawrence.

Linda said, *This is unreal. It's unheard of. I didn't even know where I was. Corridors of mirrors?*

Seeing myself in such detail. But did it make me feel good at the end. So much, I can't believe, was internally resolved for me, Robin said.

Wow, this is instant LSD…in a mirror? said Robert.

And they went on. Eric said, *This is obviously an astrologically magical, even a kind of occult, tool. This accessed my astrological makeup quite accurately. How does it do it?* Ral didn't know. Eric then asked, *The question is, How far can you go with this?* He went on, *Ral, you've been wanting to transform this world for some time. Maybe this is going to be your way of doing it. So, is this the start of a new religion? You know Joseph Smith started someway like this.*

And who was Joseph Smith? Linda asked.

Oh, he was the founder for the Mormon Church, Eric replied. And so, Eric filled them in on what Smith had found…

* * *

So now a few more friends had experienced The Mirror. The "secret circle" had now slightly increased. Were they all going to keep quiet about it? Ral and Rhonda no longer insisted on it.

Days later when a few of them did mention The Mirror to another friend, or family member, hardly anyone really believed them, or wanted to believe them, or could believe them. It was just not believable, in the way they told of the Experience, and that someone could have found such a Mirror, a Mirror, mind you, with actual magic power like that. Wasn't the friend sharing the account exaggerating a bit? It did sound occult, though. It left a few who heard about it at secondhand like this a little puzzled as to why their friend would concoct such a story. It was assumed that it was generally best to let it go.

* * *

Ral and Rhonda continued to share The Mirror with other friends who were not involved in the discussion group, and so more friends would come to visit them at their house, and they all had The Mirror Experience. It was inevitable that these friends would also begin mentioning it to others; and then a few started to share about this mysterious Mirror on social media. So, it was inevitable that this was not going to be kept secret any longer. It was most often referred to as a "magic" Mirror that a friend of theirs—often no name was given, not yet—had mysteriously found…but, again, scarcely did anyone just hearing about it at secondhand have any clear idea how that could have happened; it all sounded incredulous, like some fairytale. It would have perhaps been more believable, in some curious way, if the story had come out of, say, South America. There were always stories like this coming out of South America, or Africa, or India, or somewhere in some distant land.

At the least, a few hearing about it passed it off as being perhaps a new therapeutic technique that someone had developed from mirror gazing lore that the friend sharing would be talking about: *Look into the mirror and imagine…* But, a Mirror that had such magical properties claimed as real was just not believable. But then, an individual or two, because of the way the friend told the story, then wanted to Experience this Mirror for themselves…if, by chance, there was more to it than just a clever new form of therapy, or some new occult fad.

So, what else was being said about The Mirror Experience? Word had it that the Experience itself was said to jumpstart one into an inner journey; it could tell you things about yourself that you yourself hardly knew, and it could actually resolve inner conflicts and trigger needed changes. Though friends who had the Experience were themselves exhibiting various notable changes, did those they shared the story with really take this story seriously? When friends of the experienced friends listened to them talk about it, most of them, again, shrugged it off—it just wasn't possible—and really didn't think anything about it later; it was relegated to just hearsay and then forgotten. But a few did begin to seriously explain the story to others, and then shared it on social media, especially Facebook. So yes, more rumors about The Mirror spread, but, then, rumors and wild stories were circulating about hundreds of other things all the time anyway. Another common reaction was, *Wasn't this out of a movie?* Almost all just hearing about it as hearsay quite understandably relegated it to another exaggerated rumor. Skepticism was a given. The rumors were such that it became confusing what indeed the story really was. The almost always immediate reaction, for those who took a moment to even give it a thought, was, oh, some new mirror therapy had been started by someone, or it was some occult practice of mirror gazing that someone happened to be currently reviving. A few knew it as the old art of mirror scrying. And this was just occult lore, like Ouija boards. Though there would always be a few out there who did take Ouija boards seriously. So what else was new? New therapies and revivals of obscure occult practices were part of the contemporary cultural mix all the time. Another rumor was, it was actually some kind of hoax that someone had started.

Ral and Rhonda gave a lot of thought about how to share The Mirror with others, with many others. Rhonda, though, was not as insistent as Ral, but then they understood this perfectly: The Mirror would eventually go public. They naturally discussed it with their friends who had had the Experience. One concern was, they really didn't want a constant stream of people, even if among them were friends, coming to their house, as if some ongoing, perhaps questionable, activity was going on there that would draw the neighborhood's attention. They didn't want to rouse this quiet, close-knit, neighborhood of theirs with suspicions if lots of cars were constantly coming and going.

So then, how to go public with it? How to introduce it to others? They thought it over—no, they didn't want to set up any formal event. That would give too much the impression of trying to recruit followers to join some new group or cult. They didn't want to be known as a new version of The Two—that UFO cult back in the 70s through 90s, when Marshal Applewhite and Bonnie Nettles went around appearing at events as The Two. (The mainstream media caught up with the cult when in 1997 it made big news for a week. The cult had then taken on the name of Heaven's Gate, and on March 26 of that year (it tied into the time of comet Hale-Bopp), Applewhite and all of his followers committed mass suicide (Bonnie Nettles had died years earlier) in a town outside San Diego.) Besides, setting up an event created too many expectations—what if The Mirror suddenly didn't "perform" its "magic"? Then they would really sound like they were just trying to start up some questionable cult or even perpetrate a hoax. And imagine, too, if The Mirror Experience (as they were now calling it) did happen for everyone there? There could erupt public chaos, some people could freak out…even unpredictable hysteria could break out. Who knew what would be set off.

Rhonda and Ral had realized early on that they shouldn't keep The Mirror out of their sight; at the least, they should know where it was at all times. It was not a good idea to even go into town, which was not all that far, to the café, or to the store, or on whatever errands, and leave The Mirror behind, even if they hid it. As rumors did start to circulate, they thought it possible that someone would locate their house and break in to try to steal it. So, they had to coordinate their comings and goings to always have The Mirror close by, or to hide it in their car, if they were going out together. They wondered, were they being paranoid about this too soon?

What Ral and Rhonda and others had learned about The Mirror so far: It had become apparent early on that The Mirror Experience was not what some would be quick to assume it was, and misconceive as, instant "enlightenment." It did not offer some rarified enlightenment at all, whatever the mythically prized "enlightenment" was supposed to be, to begin with. They were intent to dispel that notion. What it actually offered was a jumpstart on the path of self-realization, a path that all who had the Experience assumed would unfold in stages. Having had the Experience, they knew that to repeatedly look into The Mirror within a short time frame was not going to accelerate one any faster through these stages; the quickly repeated Experience almost always reiterated what one had already grokked. The thing was, one had to process what breakthroughs one had made; one had to implement them in everyday life. And there was no set, predictable, timetable for when one was ready for the next stage, the next breakthrough. Yes, as what one would naturally assume, some individuals processed more quickly than others. The Mirror, strangely enough, seemed to have its own intention in these matters; and what they all discovered was this motivation, coming on as a sort of pressure, not only to share their Experience, but then how Ral and Rhonda was to share The Mirror itself. And once again, they would come to find that not everyone had exactly the same Experience that they had. But all did come away, even in a quiet altered state, with an uplifted spirit, and a wanting to work together with others.

Their friends also knew that The Mirror had potentially other powers; in fact, there was shock when the first time it happened, when The Mirror could magically increase in size to accommodate more wanting to look into it. When that happened, there was this definite aura of paranormal strangeness; the surprising shock was there that this was even happening, but everyone was soon swept into this common understanding of accepting it happening. And there was also the back of The Mirror—all the cipher script implied something more was possible with The Mirror. An Other Intelligence was obviously behind it.

Little did Ral and Rhonda know that in the middle of one night while they were asleep something new had occurred. Above their house, for about a minute, was hovering a flying saucer craft. Since it was the middle of the night, no one in the neighborhood saw anything. Now Ral for years had dreams of UFOs—flying saucers—sometimes squadrons of them. In the early 1990s he became obsessed with the whole subject of UFOs, reading almost every book on the subject. For a few years he facilitated the Santa Cruz UFO Study Group. But he himself never claimed to have had a UFO sighting.

It was time for their monthly discussion group. The write-up went out.

July's topic:

It is simply this:

What are your reflections on what

you Experienced with The Mirror?

Let's discuss this and the potential

future of The Mirror.

And let's let everyone also have another

Experience with it, if they want,

and then discuss what new Experience

you had.

At the Café

Bringing The Mirror into the public now involved another issue. Both Ral and Rhonda did start talking about it in town—they were now letting on—at the same time holding back the full story. They got frowning, quizzical looks. Something didn't sound right. And for them, it was always, what might happen if things unfolded too fast?

Ral had done some Internet research on mirror scrying, in addition to all the discussions they had had about it with others by now, so he was aware that eyebrows would be raised by those who might be practicing the art. He himself didn't know of anyone. But serious objections really, could come up. After all, wasn't this an occult practice that was performed more as a solitary ritual? One had to have a properly prepared mirror, usually having a black surface, and be psychically prepared, and take steps for a proper setting….and, above all, this was almost always done in private—usually at night, in a quiet setting, perhaps in a dimmed room, often with candles burning. This was a solitary practice for personal inner exploration. The question was, did anything truly profound happen? And apparently it also had its dangers. There were accounts of those using the practice for conjuring "demons." Stories could be read of those freaked out by the experience, left frightened, by what came alive in this often used "black mirror." Of course, it would scientifically be said that one had to believe in such so-called nonsense. It would be considered a prime example of woo-woo occultism that people rolled their eyes about, that the scientific community simply kept their distance from.

But, then, Ral's Mirror was not only no ordinary mirror, it was no scrying mirror either. So far, it was able to immediately trigger the inner journey of self-discovery for just about anyone and everyone, on the spot, without any elaborate preparations whatsoever. Again, not everyone had the same degree of self-discovery, let alone the blasting reality of a Greater Reality. And no one had any negative experiences with it at all, but all knew expressions of relief, joy, exhilaration, gratitude, and love, and to this overwhelming sense of an interconnectedness with everyone. There was this inspiring motivation to initiate cooperation with others.

Yet, Ral and Rhonda had agreed that they couldn't start with some public event. There was too much uncertainty about what that might release in a group, especially a group of strangers. They wanted to start small.

* * *

The Mirror had, soon after the discussion group, returned to its original size. Ral and Rhonda were not so surprised by that. After all, they and their friends had eye witnessed The Mirror slightly increase in size.

They contacted their friend John who had had the Experience, at least a couple of times now, and asked him if he could meet them with The Mirror at the White Raven café. He said Yes, he would. Now Ral and Rhonda were regulars at this local café in their little Santa Cruz mountain town of Felton, almost every day. It was on Highway 9 (which was not really a highway at all but a two-lane road), right smack in the middle of town, its primary business strip that still conveyed a quaint, small-town character. A curious name, White Raven. Has anyone ever seen a white raven? It was a relatively small place, with a funky, hippyish, artsy look; it only had 8 small, round tables in the front, main room, where the serving counter was on the left as you walked in. It had a smaller back room and a small rear patio. Every day the regulars would come in, no different than in thousands of other cafés around the country, around the world. Some to sit awhile and chat with others, or just to hang out awhile, others to plop down a computer and get on the Internet, and how many to write in journals; many to simply come in to get their coffee or chai and go.

Ral and Rhonda would now meet John there. Not on the weekend—there would be too many tourists at the café. So they agreed on a Tuesday, later in the afternoon, it was usually quieter then. Yes, Ral, with Rhonda, was going to bring The Mirror with them, the first time in public. John would be there in support. And it so happened that another couple of friends called them, who had not experienced The Mirror yet, and so they said that if they wanted the Experience, then come to the café on Tuesday. Who else might be there, they didn't know. And another recent acquaintance, who Ral had spoken to about The Mirror, arranged to meet them at the café for the Experience. This would be the launching of a whole new phase of The Mirror in a public space. They had to start somewhere—it was a local place, a low-key place. Since this was their favorite hangout, Ral had already generated enough curiosity among a few of the regulars—though he had been careful not to say too much, and now with rumors starting to circulate—it would be no surprise that others would be there to want to Experience what was previously just talked about. Ral and Rhonda were open then to whomever else might happen to be there who would want to take in the Experience.

* * *

Ral was always working on some project at the café; he was slowly getting to be known as a local writer and poet. Friends would know to find him there; and so many casual acquaintances were also regulars who he and Rhonda would intersect with. And the young baristas would know all the regulars too. Friends who now had experienced The Mirror, or others who heard about it, were now intent on looking for them there.

The rumors about The Mirror were only just that—rumors, secondhand hearsay. When Ral had shown up at the café some weeks that followed its discovery, others already started to approach him about what he had hinted. Yes, he himself hinted about his discovery—how couldn't he have spoken about it by now? But then, he had to keep many of these people at bay. What he would say was that the time to share The Mirror would be soon. He would soon bring it to the café and share it with others, so that just about anyone could Experience it. He also found it hard, at times, to concentrate on his many projects; but he was keeping a journal of notes about The Mirror; he knew that he would eventually have to tell its story. Life change, to say the least, was radically accelerating.

So he and Rhonda brought The Mirror to the café that afternoon. They didn't make this decision lightly. They realized they were about to step into new, unexplored, unpredictable, social territory that was on a whole other level than normal day-to-day life. But the fact was, their life had not been anything resembling normal since the day of The Mirror's discovery.

John was already sitting at one of his two favorite, centralized tables. Their other friends, an acquaintance or two, would show up shortly; one friend was Jason. The café was not that busy. They greeted John and first thought of sitting in the back enclosed patio for greater privacy, but they found there a few teenagers chatting loudly, so they turned back and had already seen that the big round table in the backroom was available. That was perfect; they could all sit around it. Ral carried The Mirror covered with a black velvet cloth, with Rhonda beside him. It didn't draw any attention from others...not yet. A few other familiar faces happened to be in the café, but they were not in on what was about to happen...not yet. John talked with both of them a bit, reviewing their Experience with The Mirror. Already there seemed, though, a heightened expectation in the air. They all had gotten their drinks by now. And so, they took seats around the big back table. Their gathering around it was to be no different than other groups that used it.

Jason, an older friend, showed up; Scott, another friend, sat with them. There was anticipation that something special was about to take place. *Okay, let's let Jason and Scott see The Mirror first*, said Ral. They certainly wanted to make sure their friends were ready. Rhonda said to both, *Just relax. Get ready to gaze into The Mirror.* John broke in, jokingly, *So you know, it's not going to be some instant psychedelic trip.* To which Jason replied *Oh?* as though this was indeed going to be something special, as he was told, but not to be compared to psychedelics. *Don't worry*, said Rhonda, *it's not going to totally freak you out. As we said earlier, we'd just like both of you to have a short Experience that'll open your eyes to who you are.*

You're kidding, I'm pretty old, Jason replied. But Jason did look a little puzzled, as did Scott; both of them now moved up closer. The two of them would view The Mirror together. And they were told again, *You're not going to freak out, stay calm.* There was now a heightening of energy in the room. John simply said, *Just wait.* And then Alex, a café regular, happened to see them and stood there, looking on. He already heard about The Mirror. *Hey Alex, you'll be next*, said Ral. Both Jason and Scott had agreed to the Experience in this public place; they trusted that there was going to be at least something to it, but not something, as they heard repeated, that would totally freak them out. Ral took off the black cloth. Alex continued to look on. The astrological symbols on the band going around it seemed hardly noticeable at first, as if they had faded. It looked at first like a simple, silver mirror, that's all. Ral didn't show them the back of it. Jason was even more curious now; how could a mirror, as they were claiming, produce some remarkable Experience on the spot like this? Rhonda and Ral hinted again not to be alarmed, this was going to be an enlightening, if startling, Experience. Their two friends were already being drawn into The Mirror.

Okay, all you need to do is gaze into The Mirror, said Ral, with John echoing, *Yes, just gaze into The Mirror. This is going to get good.* The two couldn't even turn to respond.

Ral had faced The Mirror toward both of them; it had returned to its original size. Amazingly enough, the astrological symbols became self-illuminated. Jason and Scott, like everyone else who had experienced The Mirror, were now utterly focused on it. They were riveted. There was an eerie silence around their table. Alex was increasingly curious by now. A customer or two casually walking into the room, just looking around, perhaps to check out the back patio, had to wonder what was going on, seeing this quiet group of people, and two guys staring into a mirror? Jason and Scott both kept silent, except for repeating a word to each other, *Unbelievable.* Minutes went by; they had the Experience. They soon had to get up and stand back, mouths open, but not saying anything. What could they say? Rhonda and John wondered between themselves what the two saw. They had sat back just enough not to be pulled into The Mirror. But all felt the heightened energy around it.

Alex was next; he took a seat. Ral was still holding The Mirror. Alex prepped himself to look into it; he was suddenly frozen. It was again quiet; a few minutes went by. Suddenly, he now turned away with a frown and stood up. He didn't know what to say but had to step away from the table. Everyone looked at him. A few others gathered then to take their turn. One, after gazing, remained sitting at the table, his mouth gaping. Another spoke up, *This is unbelievable! I don't know what to say,* but then, *That was me? Me?* Others had to stand up, shaking their heads, with their mouths gaping; like Alex did, they soon had to leave.

But all did ask at some point, *You found this Mirror in a pool, up in the forest?* It certainly didn't sound possible. But then, none of this sounded possible. And for that day, it was time to leave…quietly…

* * *

The next day, when Ral showed up at the café, this time without Rhonda, he didn't bring The Mirror with him; Rhonda had it at the house. Ral needed a break, that one day was enough for now. But two or three regulars approached him about it. *Hey Ral, you wouldn't happen to have that Mirror with you?* And even a stranger came up, *Oh, I hear you're the one with The Mirror. I've heard about it.* So, Ral had to say each time, *Okay, I'll have it with me tomorrow.*

So the next day Ral brought The Mirror to the café, again without Rhonda. It was busier this afternoon, and it was quite clear that a few who were there were hoping to intersect with him. The big back round table was not available; and it was almost too hot for the back-enclosed patio with others already in it on an afternoon like this. Somebody said to him, *Here's a table for you*, as it had suddenly become available; it was a table up front, in the corner of the main front window. *Sure*, and as Ral moved towards it, he got a few looks. He had The Mirror hidden this time inside a fold-out file folder, among other folders. Eyes followed the items as he put them down. He said to the person who secured the table for him, who he really didn't know, that he would first go up to the counter to order his usual shot of espresso in coffee. He then returned to the table, and at the two tables around him sat those interested in The Mirror. Alex again showed up.

Ral paused a moment, looking around. *Okay Alex, would you like to see The Mirror again?*

Ral, let the others start…talk's been going round.

One of the others said, *There's rumors going around.*

So you have it with you? another asked. Yes, he had it in the folder.

Indeed, one of the rumors was that someone was starting a hoax. For those spreading the rumors, it was not always known who the rumors were about. Just that a rumor of a local person had started it.

Ral tried to be as discreet as he could about bringing out The Mirror from the file folder and preparing those gathered around him—*don't look into it yet, and don't freak out, stay calm.* But the energy was heightened as before; he got various looks…frowns, and a sense of excitement. He then let each one there take turns gazing into The Mirror. It was still its original size. Time went by. There was the usual gasping, bewilderment. A few had to quietly leave. One of the baristas, Willow, not on shift, patiently stood close by and watched. Those who looked into it certainly got their Experience. Hands were placed on temples, eyes opened wide in complete overwhelm. *Oh my God!* was heard. Then Willow wanted to look into it. Ral said, *Sure, it's your turn now.* And so, she got the Experience and then had to stand up; she was certainly amazed and obviously brightened up—she also knew something about the occult—and could only say, *I'm glad I'm not on shift. I'll have to tell the others about this.* Rose, the owner of the café, who was not necessarily there every day, had been told about The Mirror. Willow was to tell her about her Experience with it. But Rose herself couldn't take in the Experience and still be up to conducting business. She was always busy, and always serving with the other baristas, customers. Would she take a day off to have the Experience? She wasn't sure.

Finally, Alex, who had been sitting at another table, then got to Experience it again. After only a minute or so, he said, *Enough…I got it already.* He smiled; and then he said to Ral, *You better watch your behind.* He got up and had to leave…out to the community deck…

* * *

Ral once again needed to take a break. He would not be showing The Mirror for a few days, and that meant too no one coming to the house. Rhonda agreed.

When Ral did show up at the café the following week, with Rhonda this time, he now had The Mirror with him, and there were more hoping to catch him. He had said that he would have it with him on that Wednesday.

Here, Ral, I've reserved the big table for you, old friend Bob said.

And so, a few sat around the backroom table with him and Ral. Rhonda sat at a table up front, just to watch from a distance…and to look at a magazine. Ral pulled out The Mirror once again from the file folder and first warned everyone not to look into it yet; first get relaxed, get prepared. He thought it was best that each person look into it one by one. The Mirror again complied by not increasing in size. As always, the energy was heightened.

Soon, more who happened to be in the café came forward and took their turn gazing into The Mirror. All were riveted by it, some were in silent shock. Others sitting around heard, *I can't believe this. This is unreal. Wow, did I see…* Mouths were gaping. A few had to leave. Time went by. Others in the café wondered what was going on; and those who came in to get a drink and then leave sensed too that something different, unusual, a heightened sense, was in the air. Some stood back, not really interested in the affairs of others. A few hovering around were bemused, skeptical of all the hushed excitement, thinking that someone here was just playing some mirror game. Those who looked into The Mirror at this time included an artist regular Amber, a writer who was journaling, the retired park ranger Jim (another regular), a gardener, a student, and a couple of musicians (other than Alex the musician) who always hung out. The young baristas working that day wanted to Experience it but were unable to break away and knowing by now with what they heard that it might be hours to readjust back to normal life. Some who experienced The Mirror would look at one another; they were aware. Strangers and even other regulars kept coming and going and wondered about all the serious interactions; there seemed indeed to be something strange going on.

And the word of The Mirror spread, as so many more now experienced it. Sceptics, hearing about it, shrugged it off as a local publicity stunt, a hoax that someone was trying to start, or a game involving a mirror that maybe someone found on the Internet. Was this some new woo-woo fad? Some thought that maybe this was all in reference to some movie that had just come out. It was suggested, too, that those who claimed to have had some Experience with The Mirror had been duped—the man with The Mirror was a clever hypnotist, having the skill to plant suggestions of bizarre visual journeys by simply looking at an ordinary mirror. But what those who made these suggestions failed to appreciate were the psychological changes that the experiencers were sometimes willing to share. Sometimes willing, because not everyone was about to talk openly about what psychologically transpired for them, involving personal issues about relationships, secret affairs, sexual and body complexes, anxieties, phobias, vices, etc. There was the common, quiet, self-understanding of conflicts and mental stress resolved, and relief after years of personal inner struggle. Some thought, *So this is how others must see me.* Again, not all, though, had yet the full metaphysical Experience of an unfolding Greater Reality. And no one ever walked away mad or upset; perhaps baffled, amazed, with hope, yes.

And even the occasional sceptic, after stepping forward and just glancing at The Mirror, could not resist its power—it drew the person in, and yes, the transforming Experience happened. The person was a sceptic no more.

On the Community Deck

After the third time at the café, both Ral and Rhonda realized that the growing interest in The Mirror had gotten to be too much for them to continue sharing it in its small space. For one thing, they didn't want it to interfere with normal café business. So, they decided that they would share it next on the community deck, which was only a few steps further down the sidewalk; they would now be sitting there with The Mirror. The wooden deck, with a smaller, lower deck, and a semi-perimeter bench and a couple of park tables, had been built under the massive redwood tree that was a local landmark. Sure enough, when they showed up, people found them there and gathered around. Ral, always holding The Mirror, with Rhonda sitting a little further back engaging with others while watching, welcomed those who wanted to gaze into it, usually thinking to do it at the same time. Once again, their friend John showed up; he joined Rhonda.

Suddenly there was amazement and disbelief that The Mirror remarkably increased in size to accommodate those who gathered close. Ral had to suddenly grasp The Mirror tighter.

Wow, did you see that!? Did you see that!? a young man turned around baffled, in exclamation, at no one in particular.

See what? someone on the other side of the deck, behind others, said.

Did you see what that Mirror did? It expanded, by itself!

Those who were already crammed together to gaze into The Mirror didn't quite notice, as they were now being taken by the Experience they were having; only those standing a little further back saw it happen.

A few minutes later, *Thank you! Thank you! What an Experience! It was unbelievable!* one person said. And most others who gazed into The Mirror made similar comments. They saw what they always assumed was the reality of themselves expanded in an extraordinary new light. Many entered the darkest depths of their psyche, having had no idea how deep and complex it was. One person had to immediately rush off totally overwhelmed. A few people faced one another and hugged. There were a few tears. Three musicians, Alex being one, were sitting on the lower deck, on guitars, adding to the heightened energy.

There were some, though, far on the fringes, walking by on the sidewalk, who were simply curious, thinking that this was some private gathering, and continued to walk on. Some, standing a little further back, couldn't fully see The Mirror, yet they wondered about the reactions they were witnessing. A few of those who had the Experience would tell them why all the reactions. Others walking by, seeing that a man was holding a mirror, thought he was telling a story, perhaps using it as a prop. But the question did keep coming up, *What's going on?*

Some who had the Experience walked away silently, with mouths gaping open, their eyes wide open. Rarely did they speak to those further back. They were in another world. They had to process. A few, though, walking away were noticeably rattled. A woman or two would walk away in tears. Others wanted to hug somebody.

What everyone experienced, however they reacted, had to be processed. Their Ego had to process, while it somehow had to readjust to normal reality.

* * *

It was the second day on the deck and Ral and Rhonda were greeted by many. They were sitting on the bench and at the table, waiting for The Mirror, as word had gotten around. Ral prepared for the showing of The Mirror. But, then, standing at a distance, four women together appeared to look on with suspicion; they were frowning, whispering.

They were Christian Fundamentalists who heard about The Mirror. Moments after Ral unveiled The Mirror, one of the women came up, shielding her eyes with her hand, and said, *No, I will not look into your mirror! You're practicing occult magic…it's demonic! This is a sign of the Anti-Christ!* She then made the sign of The Cross and was walking away when someone said to her, *Hey lady, what I'm getting from this is pure love.* Rhonda had watched the whole incident and was somewhat concerned.

Soon after that, while a few people began gazing into The Mirror, another woman who didn't have the Experience carefully came forward, *You know, you shouldn't be exposing people to something like this…this has unknown consequences…they have their own karma.*

Also on this day at least two people came forward to inform Ral that just recently UFOs had been seen in the sky over Felton. It hadn't made the local Santa Cruz news yet.

Yes, two of them were seen over Henry Cowell. Ral was definitely interested in hearing more. But that was all that was offered at the time.

So others came forward to gaze into The Mirror and had their Experience. The two other Johns were there, regulars on the deck. Young quiet Bodhi was there. They also gazed into The Mirror; they had the Experience. The more regular redwood deck John kept saying after, *This can't be! This can't be! This is too freaky. But I do feel good.* Bodhi had to simply walk away silently stunned and went down to the lower deck.

That was the second day.

On the third day of assembling on the community deck—Ral was there this time without Rhonda—more people were standing or sitting around. Their older friend Peter, living up in Boulder Creek, who didn't come around all that often was walking up to the deck. He quickly sensed that something was going on. Ral saw him and called out, *Peter, come on over. Do you want the Experience of your life?* There was a pause as others looked. They made way for Peter to come forward.

You know, I've had my share of experiences in life. (Indeed, Peter, rather up in age, had escaped Nazi Germany.) But Peter saw The Mirror and was curious what Ral was doing with it in front of others. Peter took a seat at the park table as one person stood up to let him sit. Ral was sitting directly across on the bench holding The Mirror.

Peter, you're going to start looking into this Mirror, said Ral. He then prepared Peter and others to start gazing into it, It was still its larger size. After a few minutes, as before, there were exclamations: *Wow! Unbelievable! I saw so much!* One person said, *I can't believe it, my childhood I saw!* Peter himself stepped away in silence; he looked serious; he was processing. He went up to Ral later after Ral had covered The Mirror to leave, having to say *Sorry* to those who didn't get to have the Experience. Peter now said, *I'm sold. This is big time. Do you know what you'll have to deal with? When word spreads about this. You have no idea what this might lead to.*

Yes, I know, Ral said.

You have something here that's unheard of. You must be careful.

Ral then explained to him how he had found it…

Shopkeepers along the strip had been wondering by now what was going on. One or two questioned if there was a permit for such a gathering, now in its third day. But the owners of the Chinese restaurant directly across from the deck showed no concern. It was not uncommon that a local sheriff officer or two would get a coffee at the White Raven. A couple of them did come out with their coffees that day and walked up alongside the wooden rim of the deck and just casually asked someone standing there what was going on.

Oh, there's someone here they say who has some magic mirror. They say it changes people.

The officers looked puzzled for a moment; they looked around; everything was peaceful, rather quiet at the moment, and so they went on their way.

But it was shortly after that that other reactions were heard:

You know this occult magic shouldn't be allowed on the deck. This needs to be practiced elsewhere…in private.

Then at one point, a couple women further back had fingers crossed; they were Christians and were aware of what was going on. One walked up closer among the others who were at the time gazing into The Mirror; she wanted to get a better idea of what exactly this Mirror looked like…and she got too close—she was close enough for just a moment. She happened to glance into The Mirror and succumbed; but only some seconds went by. Immediately she then put her hand to her mouth. She tore herself away and stepped further back and began crying. She left with her friend who was alarmed as to what happened.

Hardly anyone who glanced for even a moment into The Mirror out of curiosity had the willpower to turn away from it, so compelling was its magnetic draw. And many who heard rumors about what it could do wanted to learn more about themselves. They heard that it could cut through their childhood conditioning, their self-destructive patterns, could tame any anger they had, their suppressed hostilities… Some wanted the rumored taste of self-realization. They heard about it and now could see for themselves the joy, the euphoria, of many who now experienced The Mirror. There was this increasing wave sweeping through many of cooperation, of wanting to work together, of wanting to initiate change in the world. Everyone who fully encountered The Mirror felt that they would never say anything against it—they were irreversibly changed, transformed, in their soul, and elevated to some beginning level of enlightenment.

And something new had occurred on that third day—a man who had a physical issue of pain in his groin, who was slightly grimacing, came forward with others to look into The Mirror. He not only had his Experience, but suddenly he felt better, he felt healed, and walked away in amazement, so glad that he had come forward. And Cory, who was often a regular on the deck, still recovering from a broken ankle, suddenly received the miracle of a perfectly healed ankle after his Experience with The Mirror, Even Ral was amazed by this; it hadn't happened before. Hearing this, others had come forward and wanted to be healed…

And what Revelation were most coming to? Again, how they were all interconnected. And there was talk that The Mirror could indeed initiate change in society if it were available to a greater number of people, lots of people. There was grand talk of even changing the System. There was the question, Did this have anything to do with 2012 Mayan prophecy?

Once again, after the third day, Ral realized he could not continue meeting with people on the deck. It was arousing too much attention, the unwanted attention of suspicions, of some ferment getting beyond what he felt comfortable with at the time. Equally so, Ral and Rhonda could not handle so many new people wanting to come over to their house.

So many now were also sharing their advice. The Mirror was going to be a powerful tool not only for personal transformation, but also for social change, because the personal transformation that occurred most often now immediately translated into a recognized need for social change. And everything had to change, the System had to be deconstructed and reconstructed. As the influence of The Mirror spread, it had to be protected. The impact it was having would be challenged, attacked, opposed. Who knew what powers would want to see it destroyed…or stolen. The consensus was that they needed to form a community.

Rumors of The Mirror continued to spread locally, up and down the San Lorenzo Valley, to Scotts Valley, to Santa Cruz, in numerous ways. People were telling friends and telling their families; some were telling just about everyone they encountered. And friends and family could see such changes in those who experienced The Mirror. Many people who simply heard about it didn't know what to think; many were skeptical; and some didn't even want to hear much about it, as it was just too unbelievable…or they had religious reasons. And there were more now who wanted to Experience The Mirror for themselves. Rumors were spreading on the Internet, on social media—Facebook, Twitter, on numerous blogs… The news of the magic Mirror had not quite gone viral yet, since, especially, there was no factual documentation. It was all a matter of the direct Experience of it, otherwise it was all hearsay. Smart phone pictures had been taken of The Mirror, but they couldn't show anything. Photos could only capture the image of The Mirror; they could not convey the Experience that only human eyes were capable of.

Outside of the immediate area, it was rumored that some new religious movement, even cult, had started in the little Santa Cruz mountain town of Felton. The local sheriff department had been alerted a few times, but there was never anything further to pursue; no laws were being broken. In fact, a couple officers who were off duty had themselves the Experience of The Mirror and knew to keep a discretionary quiet about it. Though they seemed to be a little different now to the other officers they worked with, they wanted to keep their jobs. Too, the Internet chatter about The Mirror was being picked up by monitoring agencies that analyze all the myriad data that daily came across the Internet.

Friends, and suddenly so many new friends, all kept in close touch with Ral and Rhonda. Some asked if they could have the Experience again. As for their monthly discussion group, Ral sent out the topic for discussion.

> August's topic:
> Actualizing our collective dream.
> Since everyone in the group
> has experienced The Mirror
> and knows what it's capable of,
> where do we go from here
> to actualize the collective dream
> of changing society and perhaps
> even the world?

The Mirror would begin silently telling Ral things—One of the latest things The Mirror conveyed to Ral was, *Trust.* And for Rhonda, what she heard was *Keep supporting.*

And frequently, many were thinking 2012… Was this the year?

The Mirror Goes Dormant

Every week more interest in The Mirror was spreading, not only locally, but in Santa Cruz and all its surrounding areas, and even going north into Silicon Valley. Many heard about where The Mirror might have shown up in a pool and tried to locate it now. No one ever said that they had found it.

But what occurred sometime late in the summer—in September—was that a new, unexpected development took place with The Mirror. It seemed to slowly weaken, ever so slightly at first, in its ability to open its paranormal, its psychological and metaphysical, doorway. Over some weeks, Ral and Rhonda had already noticed that some change was underway. First, it appeared that the astrological symbols were fading. When The Mirror opened its dimensional doorway, scarcely did it go any deeper than a few mirrors inside of it, reflecting. What had happened to all the corridors in a labyrinth of mirrors? What happened to the labyrinth down into the soul? Here, they had assumed, after months of consistency, that The Mirror was always going to reveal its inner opening windows of deep personal insight, of transformation, of realization, of a Greater Reality. They began to feel alarmed by this. It then came to a point when The Mirror only conveyed amorphous shifting forms. Another strange thing was that the alien script on the back had changed too—it consolidated into a black circle and soon became but a black point in the center. And then one day it was as if The Mirror went dormant—it was not able to trigger any Experience;

it was simply a normally reflective mirror and had at some point gone back to its original size.

Ral was now glad that he hadn't posted anything, though the temptation was always great to do so, about The Mirror on Facebook. He had good reasons for holding back, but if he had posted about it, now he would be in the quandary of having to explain that The Mirror had become, what, just a normal mirror? So, then, what would others in the "outside" world think; what was he trying to pull off in those previous months, if he had been claiming, going on about, along with others, this "magic" Mirror he possessed? Would he be in the awkward position of having to admit that The Mirror was no longer The Mirror it was? Certainly, there were others who did post about it, giving away his name, over the months, and so Ral often got messages from others about it. He would message back that he wasn't ready to comment. So now, if there was nothing further to go on but the hearsay of old posts?

Maybe The Mirror went to sleep, Rhonda suggested. She herself would not be too concerned; she remained calm for Ral's concern. She would say, *Maybe it'll wake up one day. You know it has strange properties.* And Ral would reply, *Then maybe it's giving us time to process everything more. So much has happened so fast...*

Ever since Ral had a relationship with The Mirror, he hadn't received any channeling from his Muse, who he knew as Divine Psyche. At first, it hadn't even occurred to him, but he did start to wonder. But then, one evening, Psyche did channel to him with this simple message:

Remember, I come to you in different forms.
Remember, I am the Divine Shapeshifter.
Remember, there are phases.
Remember, there are Others in the cosmos.

And Ral did remember how She first came to him some thirty years ago in a Vision of The Fountain over Monterey Bay. In this Vision, She was shapeshifting into different figures…at the time as various Goddesses especially.

It was time for their monthly discussion group. Everyone in the group knew that The Mirror had gone dorment.

The theme for the September discussion group:

What happened to The Mirror?

But let's share what we've learned from it

and tie it into the condition of our society.

Could The Mirror have any real impact

on society if it did revive?

* * *

Not focusing on The Mirror gave Ral more time to work on his unfinished manuscripts and new poems. In particular, he wanted to finish a poetic novel that he had originally started in 1989, then abandoned it until earlier that year 2012. In a sense, it too had gone "asleep." It was titled *Lizzy Maroon Cruz'n*. Lizzy Maroon was his main character. Her name also came to him in a voice that said, *Lizzy Maroon*. He was eating lunch at a restaurant on Pacific Avenue in Santa Cruz.

Lizzy Maroon? he questioned, looking up.

You are going to write about Lizzy Maroon! the voice said. And that was it.

Why are you writing a novel in poetry? Rhonda would now ask but not to sound critical; she would say this in a loving way. *Who's going to read such a novel? Why not write a real novel that people will read? Here, we've recently gone through this amazing Experience with The Mirror that people would really find interesting to read if you were to write something about it. Make something of that—*

Ral could only reply, *Well, I probably will. But I'm just about done with Lizzy Maroon.* He definitely wanted to finish it.

And he wrote a new poem while thinking of Others out there in the universe—

Even the adult I am, I fall asleep in the arms of the stars;
such eyes watch over me & wonder as I dream—
The Ever-Awakened Ones, they are far wiser than my years—
I am still a child upon this Earth;
but I too shall awaken in time,
I too shall awaken in time…

* * *

So what could they now do about The Mirror? As they always did now, they wrapped The Mirror in a fine silk cloth; it went into a cleared-out drawer of his clothes bureau, large enough for the original size Mirror. Every day for weeks, they took The Mirror out and looked at it. One of them would always say, *Let's take a look at The Mirror.* But nothing seemed different about it.

Sometime later in the fall, though, they did notice that a change had occurred—The Mirror appeared to be now slightly encrusted, as if it had been corroded by sea water, as if, what, it had been in the ocean for years? So, The Mirror could indeed still change! But what were they to think of this development?

By this time, as the months went by, the rumors about The Mirror began to fade, and to a great extent came to an end. Those who did get the Experience months ago often asked Ral or Rhonda about it—*what's the latest?* The mostly hearsay memories of some, quote, "magic" Mirror that someone had claimed to have found sank back into the cultural void, so that they were simply forgotten in the constant shuffle of Postmodern culture that bombarded everyone with dozens of different stories every week.

Ral sometimes remembered his large Moon mirror from years ago, when he lived up on the mountain above Aptos. He had accidentally cracked it when he was moving it around; he wasn't paying attention to where he had placed it, so it slipped, fell over on the floor, and cracked. He and Rhonda—after she had moved into his studio on the mountain—would still use it though in the same position it had, resting on the back of a cushioned chair. He had once taken a surreal-like photo of the two of them looking into it at that time. But the two pieces of cracked mirror at one point separated from its backing, and shortly after, it all came apart. It was about the same time that they had to move off the mountain. Ral remembered the two fragments of the mirror piled outside of his place, and the bare plywood circle backing that he now had no use for; he completely forgot what became of it all.

Ral remembered his relationship with the Moon. He remembered his long nights of working when he would watch the Moon night after night, going through its phases, month after month. It was the lesson of change, and the lesson of inspiration coming and going. As the soul changed, as water changed, as Nature changed—he took that as a Moon lesson.

The October and November discussion groups again brought up The Mirror and what its potential might have been, or if it... Rhonda was always to say, *Maybe it's gone to sleep and hopefully will wake up.* The others by now were not so sure; maybe it was some cosmic fluke, forever to be a mystery. But they all realized the positive changes that The Mirror had initiated for them. By November, however, the focus was more on recent developments in the culture, society, out there in the world...

It was then December's monthly discussion group topic:
December 21st, here we come—
After all these many years that date

Dec 21, 2012 has been referenced
in the culture and referenced in our
own discussions—
The Mayan calendar focused on it
with prophecy. Is anything about
to happen for us globally?
Here we are, with that date now
upon us in about a week.
On the same note, this day of our meeting,
the 13th, sees planet Uranus going
stationary direct in square aspect
to Pluto, with the Moon coming
into conjunction with Pluto.
Whatever has been held back for months
is now about to be released as Uranus
in Aries is now given the go-ahead
to initiate, and now the Moon too
might possibly be a trigger on that
very day. A potential for suddenly
activated release for change, big time
change, is certainly there. Eric plans
to be here, so he will also offer
his own astrological perspective.

There had been all the buildup, the hoopla, the culture media circus, all the prophecy projections, all anticipations of the day December 21, 2012. Their discussion group was to focus on it, but they all assumed there was not going to be some Big Event on that day. They all assumed that December 21 would come and go with nothing extraordinary happening.

* * *

It was the New Year of 2013. Living up in Felton, Ral and Rhonda had often driven down to the coast, usually finding themselves in Santa Cruz first and then often cruising along West Cliff Drive, or sometimes they went up the coast to Davenport or all the way up to Half Moon Bay. So, one day they were down at the cliffs overlooking the great Pacific Ocean. Ral parked his car, they got out and walked the few steps to the edge of an ice plant bluff, above the big, jagged boulders awash in the tide of the surf. They gazed out over the ocean. They had been following the Fukushima nuclear reactor story of its disaster closely since early in 2011 and thought of the radiation leaking into the Pacific every day. They thought of the death-making radionuclides killing off marine life, how long the radioactive fan would take until it eventually reached the West Coast. There was great concern among some that Fukushima could eventually kill the Pacific Ocean and eventually contaminate the entire biosphere.

Over the years Ral occasionally had dreams of standing at, or walking alongside, or driving alongside, the edge of the ocean…and sometimes even a flying dream where he flew a short distance out over the ocean. The feelings he had in these dreams were often unsettling, even frightening; there was about the ocean such an enormous living presence so close that it could swallow him. But it was not the danger of actually drowning that he felt, but the overwhelming enormity and alien unknown of the ocean. One night, though, years ago, his dream was of a large mirror that was being hauled out of the ocean; there was machinery, cranes, ropes…it was brought up onto the beach...and people were looking into it. Who knows what they saw. He seemed to recognize this mirror…and water was flowing all around it or seemed to be coming out of it. He got close and saw a huge cavern, or was it a canyon, open up in it. It was uncanny how that dream mirror was a premonition of The Mirror opening to the depths within.

It was also during this time that Ral did go up into the forest where he had found the pool and The Mirror down inside of it. He looked around and looked around, believing that he retraced his steps to the best of his memory. But no, he didn't find it. And he never heard of anyone finding it, though a number of people had looked for it…

The Mirror Revives

Some months had gone by. Every day, friends and others, were always approaching Ral and Rhonda about The Mirror, especially at their hangout, the café. *Anything new? Anything different about it?* And they had to keep saying to everyone *No.* There was the usual disappointment.

Their discussion group no longer focused on The Mirror but returned to topics they had usually focused on in the past. Topics such as: What is your life about? (Certainly, their Experience with The Mirror came into that discussion.) What is humanity about? The future of creativity. Are we evolving? Your place in society. Our sense of community. What about mainstream media? Is civilization nearing an Edge? The stories about ETs.

It was during this time that UFOs were being sighted again in the area. Ral and Rhonda didn't always see them, but they got word of the sightings from others. It was even brought up in their local San Lorenzo Valley monthly paper. They didn't realize, as once before, that a faintly glowing flying craft would hover over their house at night. But, as years ago at night, Ral had UFOs coming up in his dreams. Even squadrons of UFOs flying above. One short dream he remembered in some detail. It went: He was standing outside somewhere with a man standing next to him; it was night. A bright full Moon was in the sky. Ral said to him, *Look at that Moon!* Suddenly the man was no longer standing at his side, but Ral saw that the Moon now changed into a flying saucer. It started moving down to the left and was shrinking in size. It was coming further down, still shrinking. To the left of Ral was an outside bar for sitting, as some restaurants would have. He rushed to the bar and put his opened hands on its surface. The flying saucer, still descending, had shrunk so much in size that it now landed in his open hands. He said to it, *Help me! I will do anything!* He suddenly awoke.

Ral was inspired at that time to write a short poem:

The UFO

> It confounds human intellect,
> stretches any boundary we select;
> it comes and goes at will,
>   and still,
> it profoundly preserves its secrecy—
> To our past and to our future,
> it is the enigmatic key.

Everyone who had The Mirror Experience always assumed that some Other Intelligence was behind it. So Ral was inspired to write another poem in a more direct style:

Who?

> Who planted this Mirror?
> Who are They?
> Was it for me to find?
> Was it for us to realize
> there are Others,
> Others in the universe
>   out beyond?
> Was it for us to learn
> to take the next step,
> the next stage,
> in our human evolution?
> Others are watching

over us,
holding secrets of our reality
we cannot today comprehend—
Someday—hopefully—we will

comprehend.

* * *

It was sometime later in the spring that Ral opened the drawer that contained The Mirror, as he always did, to check on it. He uncovered it and now noticed a change was occurring. He quickly brought it out and held it. A dramatic change: It appeared that The Mirror had come alive. Ral saw water flowing around the rim of The Mirror, the rim where the astrological symbols had previously appeared. He saw tiny flowing rivulets, and he immediately saw that at the top—what he took to be the top—of The Mirror, the rivulets, which were too like flowing hair, were coming from a fountain. It was as if a Living Fountain was pouring around The Mirror; and he noticed that the water cleansed The Mirror of the slight encrusted discolor that had occurred over the months. His fingers did not even get wet, and he noticed further that however he turned The Mirror, The Fountain would always indicate the top. The rivulets flowing over the face of The Mirror didn't allow him to see his reflection in it just yet.

Ral rushed to the doorway of his room with The Mirror in his hands and called down the hallway to Rhonda, *Rhonda, what we've been waiting for— The Mirror has come alive!*

She didn't hear him; she was downstairs. He looked: The Fountain was still flowing. Now he turned it over. The central dot that had been there for months had radiating lines, lines that looked to be activating.

He rushed to bring The Mirror downstairs, and before he could see Rhonda, he was again exclaiming, *The Mirror has come alive!*

Now she came out of the kitchen and entered the hallway. He showed it to her, and she looked and marveled at what she saw.

Aha, she said. *What did I say months ago? The Mirror had gone to sleep.* Rhonda was so pleased that she had been right. But then, would The Mirror fully revive to again offer its Experience? The Fountain was still flowing. They watched.

Yes, moments later replied Ral, *and remember what I suggested the reason was…it wanted to give us some time to process. The Mirror has a mind of its own.* And then he quickly said, as they had been watching what was happening, *Do you see that it's The Fountain? The Fountain that I've been talking about all these years? The Fountain that's apparently reviving The Mirror.*

Yes, waking it up, Rhonda replied.

And how long would it keep flowing around The Mirror like that? A short time went by… Soon, they were relieved—The Mirror appeared to be fully awake again. They were already sitting in the living room. Ral was still holding it; they both looked into it. Yes, they could see the corridors of mirrors going into their psyches as before. They sat there, entranced. They felt a great sense of renewal. And now, that Greater Reality that had been opening before was gaining more clarity—they suddenly saw a galaxy of stars, stars with planets…they saw flying saucers and huge, long cigar flying craft. They looked at one another; Ral placed The Mirror down on the living room table. They hugged. They kissed. A premonition…

Well, it's awake for us again, Rhonda said. *A new chapter for us begins…*

Ral got on the phone and called the four friends who first experienced The Mirror:

Well, gosh, said Henry, *the magic has come back.*

John said, *Good news. I'll be down.* (He lived in Bonny Doon.)

Erin said, *This was meant to be. You always hoped this would happen.*

Paula said, *Well well. All this time you two were waiting for this…*
And Ral would enigmatically say to himself, *I will go where The Mirror takes me…*

And so, The Mirror returned to its former life. It was again The Mirror that opened to all the inner realms of the psyche, and that revealed a Greater Reality breaking through, revealing other worlds, flying craft between worlds. The Ahh! of experiencing it had returned. They contacted more friends over days. A few of them showed up at their house to confirm for themselves that The Mirror had revived. Yes, indeed it had. They were hesitant, though, to say anything yet out in the public. For now, they kept quiet in their usual hangouts, especially the café. But it was somewhat difficult. They wanted to give themselves some time to process this new development.

One day, they were given notice by the owner of their house. They could no longer continue living there. Yes, they were renters, and the owner wanted the house back for his family; so, they were given a typical two-month notice. They wondered, though, if the owner had previously heard something about The Mirror that made him concerned. Coincidentally, Ral now had limited funds at this time. So, what were they to do? But their friend Peter, who had his Experience of The Mirror back on the community deck, upon hearing about this recent chain of events from Ral, soon after contacted them. He immediately stepped in and offered them a residence on his property in Boulder Creek, as he had a couple of cabins on it, besides his house, that were not currently being rented. Was that merely a coincidence? They also talked about the possible start of a small community there. It would have to be small; Peter didn't have all that much property. But they thought, sure, it would be a community of The Mirror.

The Early Community

Peter had always been a fan of Ral's work. He collected his recently published titles. (Finally Ral was publishing.) He believed in The Mirror and was quite willing to start a small community. Small—he didn't want to be overwhelmed. His property was somewhat of a clearing in the common wooded area of Boulder Creek. Tall redwoods surrounded, and tall firs. Peter's house was not far from the cabins; his Japanese wife Koi didn't venture out that much; she was quiet, not especially a talker. Her primary outings would be to always go with Peter into town. She only once decided to Experience The Mirror. After, she had quietly gone back to their house. She told Peter later in so many words she had to process. As well, Peter renewed his Experience. It confirmed that a small community was wanted.

During the day The Mirror would be mounted in a wooden frame for viewing. The Mirror had again enlarged a bit. So, it was not very large, yet larger than when Ral first found it. At night, it would be brought into Ral and Rhonda's cabin, covered.

They all realized, though, that the property, a couple of acres or so, had its limitations. It was not as if they were able to accommodate any interest expressed by others in a larger commune; it would only be about twelve people. Those who wanted to stay on the property would set up weather-proof tents or reside in RVs and motor homes; the other cabin was quickly taken. Visitors were welcome, and, of course, were always showing up to Experience The Mirror. And word soon got out that healings were again taking place. Everyone in Boulder

Creek soon knew about The Mirror. So, it was agreed that two or three times a week, visitors would be welcome to come onto the property and undergo the Experience. Sometimes they allowed small groups to visit. The one rule was that if one came to the property, whether alone or with others—and often these were strangers to one another—that one had come to Experience The Mirror, and not to cause any problem. You never knew what ulterior motive someone might have. There was no just casual visiting, except for the few friends that Ral and Rhonda and others in the community had. They already intuited, as The Mirror continued to reveal so much, that outside infiltrators would want to spy on them and perhaps bring in another agenda and create discord. For word about The Mirror was again spreading.

And one day, an incident did occur: A young man who parked his car outside the property came storming in. He didn't get very far. Steve, one of the residents who lived there, who often stood at the entrance to the property, saw him.

Wait! Stop! You can't just run in like that! Steve yelled. But the young man was rushing around. Steve called out to others nearby. Another resident, and a visitor, rushed up; the three of them tried to confront the young man. But they ended up having to wrestle him down. *That goddamn mirror needs to be stopped!* He was spouting incoherently about UFOs, End Times, Jesus is coming... The three had to calm him down and told him that he had to leave. They weren't about to call the sheriff; they didn't want this to go any further. The three got the guy up and fortunately he left, still muttering. Ral and Rhonda happened to be in town at that time; Peter and his wife were also in town. They all then heard about the incident when they returned.

The community was also wary of those who might possibly want to steal The Mirror, which is why they had to always keep an eye on it, and hidden in Ral and Rhonda's cabin after daylight. But all it took, as before, was a direct glance at it. That one glance was it for any evil intention to be dissolved. And usually, two or three in the community would always be circling around the property, as word about The Mirror continued to spread, even further now. Everyone in the San Lorenzo Valley, down again in Felton, knew about it, with many showing up to have the Experience. But the word about it was spreading much further.

And what revelation was everyone who experienced The Mirror now coming to? Again, not everyone had exactly the same Experience. Some experienced primarily their inner psyche dynamics. Everyone saw into their psyche and saw the mirrored corridors of their own inner drama. They saw corridors of their conflicts, confusion, pent up anger, their complexes and struggles… And these personal issues were resolved for everyone…fears no longer made sense, the anxiety of alienation vanished. Conditioned Ego concerns—always this Me Me Me were blasted and scattered; no more this need to self-aggrandize, no more greed, competition was a boring game…no need for power struggles. Again, this was not some instant enlightenment, but the beginning of a process of self-discovery happening in the moment that could also be the revelation of a Greater Reality, of other stars, of other worlds. So, the psyche changes were more than personal for some; but there were no judgements being made. The Ego of Me Me Me began to see how they were all interconnected and interdependent. It hit not as an abstract idea that one could entertain to debate, but as a moment-to-moment new way of being with one another. It was a process now fully conscious. All felt such a tremendous love for all life, a compassion for all. All now realized their Path in life, as many were uncertain before as to what their life Path was. Ral often said that once finding one's Path, live it consciously and passionately. Reenter the world with greater confidence, with a mission.

In their bathroom, Ral would now be looking into *its* mirror and asking himself *Who is this?* He found himself then writing a poem about what he was experiencing looking into the bathroom mirror:

Is that me?

I look in this mirror—
Who is this looking back at me?
That's me? Is that me?
Is that this person I look like?
    Wait a minute.
Is that the person who in The Mirror
is going multidimensional,
whose psyche is self-actualizing
    into a Greater Reality,
who is an open door to Other Intelligence,
who channels the coming-to-us
    of Divine Psyche?
Is that one, single face in this mirror me?
    Can it be me?
Should I frown? Should I smile?

* * *

The discussion group, unfortunately, had to come to an end. Not everyone in the group wanted to drive up to Boulder Creek. Besides, there were no big tables and not enough chairs; Ral and Rhonda's cabin was too small for a group. The same for the other occupied cabin. And Peter was not so inclined to having a big group in his rather small house. The members in the group had had the Experience and a few would show up at some point to have it again.

They were all trying to decide on a plan for getting The Mirror out to more people, and to people who might desire to Experience it again for their further psychospiritual development, not to mention, any physical healing. But how exactly could they do that? Would it again be some public venue? Again, they all knew that Peter's property was limited in what it could accommodate. Peter would say, *Well, I know about my property. What can I say?* The others there didn't worry about or complain about it. They were all one getting along family.

Now one day a man parked outside and stepped out wearing a suit at the entrance to the property. Steve and Donna were there, as one or two were now always on "duty" at the entrance. The man said to them, *No, I'm not here to see The Mirror at this time. But I'm here to share with all of you that I have exciting plans for it. I can pay big money for its use. I can easily promote it in the media. I have a team of marketers. I can do more. Perhaps a documentary. Who do I talk to?*

Steve and Donna were taken aback. Steve had to say bluntly, *I don't think so.* Donna simply responded, *Marketers? Huh? Are you kidding?*

And then Steve asked, *How did you hear about it?*

Well, the word about it is out there, the man said.

Really, that much? replied Steve.

At that moment Rhonda happened to come by. Steve said to the man, *Here, talk with her—*

So, what's up? Rhonda asked, looking at the man dressed in a suit. She had a frown. Donna said, *This guy wants to put money down to take The Mirror places…the media…perhaps a documentary.*

Rhonda looked at the man. He looked at her. *Yes, can I help you?* Rhonda asked.

So you're the one to talk to?

Well, yes, Rhonda replied.

Then the man went on about how he and his marketing team up in San Francisco heard about The Mirror and that he and his team could promote The Mirror big time, with big money down. Rhonda was shaking her head. She then replied, *Do you realize what this Mirror can do? It can promote itself. We don't need outside help of your kind.*

But he went on, and they went back and forth for a few minutes, with Steve and Donna listening. Rhonda finally convinced him that the answer was *No.* The man left disappointed. Rhonda said to Steve and Donna, *Wow, was he naïve.* And so, they all realized that more word about The Mirror was getting out there.

So often visitors brought cameras and video cameras with them; cell phones were common. But they could never capture the inner worlds that The Mirror revealed, only the external, visible Mirror.

And all this time now, UFOs were again coming around, usually at night. Those living there didn't often see them for all the trees in the dark, but they did occasionally show up during the day. They all knew that Others were aware of them, watching them. And did Others from elsewhere have a greater plan for them? They all discussed this frequently…

A Larger Community Begins

A most remarkable development now occurred. One night, The Mirror had again magically of its own enlarged itself even more. It was always placed covered on a table set aside for it every night in Ral and Rhonda's cabin. It now had expanded across the whole table and more. The covering over it was not enough. Fortunately, it was centered on the table. Upon awakening, Ral and Rhonda were startled to see it. *What?* But then, it had done this before, but not this large. When they both carried it outside, everyone saw that it was now a much larger Mirror, not quite as large as both hands outstretched. Everyone stood around amazed.

Rhonda said to everyone, *I think The Mirror is telling us something.*

Yes, Rhonda, I think so, someone said.

Yes, this is certainly a new development, said Ral, And others had to agree.

Someone grabbed a camera to document the larger Mirror; a few cell phones were also brought out…

Peter, of course, saw The Mirror that morning. He was somewhat puzzled about what to do now. For one thing, it would now seem no longer possible to keep it in a small community on his property. All in the community agreed and wondered what to do next. Peter had to think it over; he wanted to go into town. A new frame was made for The Mirror. Days then went by; a couple of weeks went by. It was already late summer…

Then, one day, a man who heard about The Mirror—as news was now spreading further afield about it—who lived in the California Central Valley showed up to see firsthand what this Mirror was all about. He often liked to visit the Bay Area since he was originally from San Jose. (He moved to the Central Valley with family money.) Boulder Creek was a little out of the way, down in the Santa Cruz area, but he often liked to come down to Santa Cruz anyway. And for something like this, he didn't mind at all. Gavin heard about The Mirror through the grapevine and a local offbeat news report in nearby Modesto. He happened to own many acres of property in the farmland of the Central Valley. Because he was still evaluating his property, he hadn't planted any crops yet, and it had gotten too late in the season anyway. Was there a bigger picture here that he was not conscious of? The thing was, he was always curious about the unusual, about strange events, so that one day he decided to drive down to Santa Cruz, up to Boulder Creek, where the community was. In town, he asked about the property where The Mirror was located. Those in Boulder Creek certainly knew all about it. So, there was really something to this, he thought. Given directions, he then found his way to Peter's property and was welcomed by a community member standing at the entrance. Like so many others, he explained that he was there to see The Mirror. And he was there on a lucky day when they were open to visitors. At the moment, he was the only one. Ral and Rhonda were there and greeted him as he came walking up toward where The Mirror was mounted. A few chairs were always available.

He was told, Now get yourself centered and remain calm. Gavin had no problem with that; he was always level-headed and calm. Ral and Rhonda watched as he sat before The Mirror… Minutes went by and he soon had the full Experience alright. He was an unassuming, modest man, always willing to help others. And he suddenly felt that he could do more. He turned his eyes from The Mirror and turned to the side, quietly amazed…so much amazed, like everyone. No one bothered him. Everyone knew to wait for a person to be ready to talk. After a short time, he stood up and started talking with the others who were there, including Ral and Rhonda, and said, *This is unbelievable. What can I say, it did happen. There is nothing that I'm aware of in the world that comes close to this. I'm so glad I made the effort to get here.* He was soon told that this small community could no longer accommodate any more people, especially now that The Mirror had increased in size. Gavin's willingness to help others was indeed enhanced by the Experience. He turned to Ral and Rhonda and surprised them—he would offer his land for a larger community. It was in the Central Valley, not that far from Modesto. So, they immediately started talking about making plans and would also inform Peter and his wife who were in town at that time. Peter would feel relieved.

Over a few weeks a migration would be underway. Ral and Rhonda had first driven out to the Central Valley to meet with Gavin. He said when they arrived, *Welcome to the Land. I hope this works out.* They then surveyed his property for what it offered. Besides his own house, he did have a cabin available. They told Gavin that this was a great opportunity, that it would work. Ral and Rhonda then returned to Peter's community and said that it was a go. Most in the first community would now make plans to move to the Central Valley. Gavin would welcome them all; they would all be considered as one family. It took a few weeks, though, to coordinate everyone and make it happen, as people were on different schedules and had to think about living arrangements, if it seemed necessary.

Gavin again greeted Ral and Rhonda when they now arrived in a van that could accommodate the now larger Mirror. (They had been gifted with purchasing the van by a well-off visitor who had the Experience.) Gavin again showed them the cabin that they would live in. They also located the best place on his property for mounting The Mirror. They decided it would not be that far from the entrance; the outer surrounding property would be set aside for community members to settle on. Another frame for it was soon made by those who knew carpentry. After that was done, it was taken out of the van and mounted…

People from around the state were now hearing more about The Mirror and this new community that settled around it, and many started showing up. The community started with about 30 permanent/semi-permanent members. Not everyone who showed up over time were planning on joining the community but were obviously there to have the Experience that they had heard about. Sometimes families would show up; it was advised that children were too young to encounter The Mirror. (More often those who had children or teenagers would have them stay with friends or relatives.) In the early days, there was enough land for everyone who wanted to settle there. People either set up weatherproof tents or had motor homes and RVs. Then, even a couple more cabins would soon be built. There would be no fencing around the property and no gate, but of course there was the drive-in entrance way. There were a few radios and televisions that could pick up local stations. Internet connections for computers were also made. Those in the community always shared everything. No one went without. They all felt interconnected. And often people visiting would contribute to the community, whether it was money or food, supplies, or other items, Ral was inspired one day to write a poem about the greater connectedness of everything:

Connectedness

Every star, every blade of grass—
Connectedness.

Every heartbeat, every breath, every kiss—
Connectedness.

Those who play the game of separateness
play unwittingly in a much larger game—
Connectedness.

There is no escape—
Love or hate, hit or miss,
it is one vast extended
Inter-*c o n n e c t e d n e s s.*

* * *

There were always three or so members at the makeshift entry to the property who greeted those who arrived. The greeting was most often, *Welcome to your new life.* And those who arrived would soon find out what that implied.

And it was soon after everyone had settled in, with many too always coming and going, that highly unusual events started happening. First, UFOs—definite looking flying saucers—were being seen hovering around the community and in the wider area, most often at night. The community soon came to expect them. A few posted about it on social media but there was still no rush to tell all the world. Yet, the word of sightings did start spreading. Even the government back in Washington DC would eventually start to hear about them. Jets were sometimes seen in the sky, monitoring the area. And as more word got out, media reporters would show up and would want to get details about The Mirror and the UFO sightings. Occasionally one of them would want the Experience. Marketing agents for video shows on the Internet would also show up. Those at the entranceway would try to satisfy them regarding what they wanted to know. Often Ral and Rhonda came forward and were interviewed. And however much money would be offered, The Mirror would not be taken off the property.

Community members would always be watching the night sky. The area they lived in was always clear, bright starry clear. The star multitudes would keep them aware: Yes, Others were out there. The UFOs, the distinct flying saucers they saw, confirmed that. And what they saw in the night sky would remind many of what they saw in The Mirror. They also followed the Moon, the phases of the Moon. Its phases also reminded them of their own inner and life phases. They also kept track of the brightest of Venus and Jupiter, and of Mars.

And one day the most remarkable of all events happened: In broad daylight a rather large flying saucer appeared above the community. Seeing it, everyone marveled. It then slowly descended and apparently would be landing. Quickly everyone scattered out of the way; it softly settled on the ground. Those who happened to be the nearest gathered before it, including Ral, Rhonda, and Gavin. They all stood there, staring at it. Hands went to mouths gasping; Ral and Rhonda held hands, as did a few other couples. Gavin quietly said, *Welcome to the Land.* And Rhonda: *Here we go again.* Other exclamations were heard. Ral squinted his eyes and said, *It's happened.*

A camera was quickly brought out; a few cell phones showed up. Moments later, a door slid open. A woman stepped out on a platform that unfolded; she was tall, slender, with long, white, almost glowing hair. She was of course wearing an outfit meant for space travel. She looked at those who were gathered in awe, and announced,

I am Kaila of the Galactic Federation. We are aware of you and your Earth. We are aware of The Mirror. You will be using this Mirror to transform your world. Your world is in trouble. Alarming developments are happening. Events that are endangering all of you and your world. Nations aggressive, facing off with one another for control, for war. Nuclear weapons could destroy your global civilization, could annihilate humanity.

Your Earth is changing. It will be up to you humans to transform your world into an enlightened world. The Mirror will continue to teach you. She saw Ral and blinked her eyes.

Someone now called out, *Is the Galactic Federation behind The Mirror?*

Kaila smiled and seemed to nod her head. She said, *I will return.*

She turned around to reenter the ship; it lifted off. Yes, word of this spread far and wide. It would only be the beginning...

So Ral, Rhonda, and their first friends who experienced The Mirror were correct all along in their assessment that some Other Intelligence had to be connected with The Mirror. An intense discussion among many of the community members began…

Other surprise occurrences started happening. Often what looked like Hindu gurus, Zen masters, Ascended Masters, were seen in almost transparent form hovering just above the ground. Just about everyone could see them. And a few persons claimed they saw who they took to be Jesus hovering likewise. By now the community would not be shocked by these new events. They came to accept that their world was in the process of radically changing.

One early evening as Ral and Rhonda were stepping out their door, this semi-transparent figure was hovering right in front of them. They held hands. Yes, like those who claimed to have seen before, its face immediately reminded them of the image of Jesus. The hovering figure spoke, just three words: *Remember…My Love.* The figure then faded. Rhonda and Ral had to hug one another. They shared what they saw and heard with a few who happened to be not far. They would share it with everyone the next day.

And other developments of the natural world were occurring. Birds had started coming around much more regularly and in numbers. Song sparrows singing were now more common in the community. Blackbirds, grackles, crows, waxwings, towhees, bluebirds, magpies, scrub jays, were all showing up, totally unafraid of coming so much closer to those in the community. And a sparrow hawk was frequently observed hovering overhead. Oh yes, the sparrow hawk was Ral's symbolic personal bird going back to his teenage years when he was an avid birdwatcher. He would always gaze up at it in those years when it came around…as he did now. And most unusual was a raven that would occasionally perch on the upper frame of The Mirror. It would Aaahhhk! Aaahhhk! down to anyone who was close. Ral also could not help but remember that back in Felton on the community deck, a raven would perch on a light pole above and Aaahhhk! Aaahhhk! down to the deck. And Ral would reply in turn; back and forth they would go. Was some other psychic plane accessing his psyche? And this would be true for others regarding the hovering figures recently seen— How many community psyches were being accessed?

And deer would come much closer into the community. Wild turkeys too, Foxes would show up, seemingly wanting attention. Rhonda would say, *I sense that Nature wants—needs—our help*. And others had to agree.

And on another day the most remarkable thing happened—out of The Mirror flew monarch butterflies, hundreds of them. How was that even possible? Those standing around were totally amazed. But then, they all realized that anything was now possible. The monarchs flew throughout the community, even landing on people. The energy in the community was certainly getting heightened.

It was just over a week later that Kaila returned with her ship. Again, she stood out on a platform. This time steps unfolded to the ground. Ral and Rhonda were standing to the front of those who had now gathered. Kaila said,

I am here to take a few of you on a tour into your galaxy. The Mirror has given all of you the psychic Experience of what you have called a Greater Reality. Now this Experience can be taken to a whole new level—a full

reality Experience. Who would take this exploration with me? Have no fear, you will return here, to Earth, to your community.

Those closest to the craft turned and looked at one another. Everyone was dumbfounded. Who would step forward? It was assumed that Ral would take up her offer. He looked at Rhonda. She said, *You go. You will share with us what you experience when you return.* Gavin was in town at that time.

So Ral and ten others stepped forward. Kaila welcomed them to take the steps up to the ship. They took the steps and the next moment they entered the ship. Once inside, Kaila said to Ral, *I am aware of you already.* He blinked. He and the others now inside were totally taken aback. It was huge inside the ship, so much larger than it looked on its exterior. Was this an optical illusion? And the flashing, pulsing lights surrounding the ceiling, the long instrument panels... And then suddenly an android appeared and stood at one panel...

There was a subtle sensation that they were lifting off. They had no idea that they were already in the upper atmosphere. Suddenly a window appeared. Kaila motioned for them to go to it. Ral and the others went to it and could see the Earth, the noted Blue Marble once described by an astronaut, already far below... Earth was soon shrunk, tiny in their view, in the vastness of black space. The millions of stars were so much more brilliant than they looked on Earth. Their Sun had soon become but another star. Kaila said to them,

Your space program is only in its infancy. Realize, we are going to different worlds. There are over three trillion planets in our galaxy. Your Sun is only one of two billion stars in this galaxy. No longer will your humanity wonder of the possibility of different worlds. Here I am, with you, from another world. It is time that humanity opens up to Other Intelligence, other advanced civilizations. You will view a few other civilizations in this galaxy of ours. The Mirror gave you but a mental experience. Now will see with your own eyes.

How fast the ship was going, they had no idea. The humans were told they would be entering a time tunnel. Suddenly outside the window looked blank; there was a slight sensation felt. Seconds went by…the window was again clear. And so soon they approached a star becoming as bright as the Sun; so soon they were nearing a planet in its system. They flew into its atmosphere and lowered in elevation to where they could see the rugged ground but then open spaces, and trees and vegetation. Kaila said that here was an example of a people who had not yet reached a state of civilization. Their craft lowered enough and hovered. And who were these hairy, strange looking people? Those looking out the window indeed saw no sign of civilization. The figures they saw looked up at their craft and raised their hands and lowered their hands. They did it again. What—or who—did they see this craft was?

They then flew over other planets with civilizations, civilizations the equivalent of what human civilizations looked like in history, including current humanity. They quickly flew over the latter. The most notable they flew over was a futuristic city with tall, slender spired buildings on the shore of an ocean; they saw an arching bridge to an island that also had a few spired buildings. They saw flying craft in the air among the buildings, coming and going. Then, two flying saucer craft suddenly appeared outside their window. Kaila told them not to be alarmed; this civilization was a member of the Galactic Federation; the approaching craft were just acknowledging them. As they left this planet, she also said there were civilizations that were threatening, that would want to dominate other planets. Their people had not yet realized an enlightened state. What would it take? Perhaps a Mirror?

Kaila said to them, *This is only our galaxy. You saw only a few of the many civilizations in our galaxy. Realize there are over a trillion galaxies in the universe. I will tell you more of what the Greater Reality implies.*

Kaila again said to Ral aside from the others,

I was aware of you already. Then, *There was a reason you found The Mirror. We planted The Mirror in that pool. And I am aware that you know that you live in a sick, endangered world. That will have to change.*

Ral had a private suspicion that Kaila had telepathic ability. And Kaila could immediately grok that. Then Kaila told them all,

I came to your planet as a relatively human-looking woman. You and your people would relate. But on my planet, there is no duality of men and women, as you humans would say. Our people can change their bodies however they choose.

As they were returning to Earth, Kaila got philosophical and said to them,

You will come to realize there are multidimensions. There are other universes. Realize that your philosophical notion of Being implies an Unlimited Potential and Unlimited Manifestation.

With his philosophical background Ral understood, while the others just accepted what she said. Telepathically, Kaila knew that about Ral.

Upon their return to Earth and to the community, they received a surprise—those in the community who happened to be in front of The Mirror, with others then suddenly gathering at The Mirror, witnessed in it the cosmic adventure that Ral and the others had experienced. They too experienced it in The Mirror. Everyone was realizing that an altered, what they knew as sci-fi, reality was now constantly taking place for them. In fact, it became unnecessary for Kaila to return again to take others into space. A full-on three-dimensional virtual reality Experience of the galaxy was available when others consciously wanted it, standing before The Mirror.

Kaila last said to them, *You have seen other worlds. We of the Galactic Federation wish not to see your human race fail.*

And there were other developments: There were a few remote viewers in the community whose ability to see other places was enhanced. The one place, in particular, that those few with concern could zero in on was the federal government back in Washington. They began warning the community that the government was up to something regarding The Mirror and the community.

And telepathy was also being gifted in others. For Ral and Rhonda, it was primarily their ability to see into one another.

People from around the country were increasingly showing up. People with various backgrounds, but especially those with backgrounds that were metaphysical, spiritual, and occult. Not only that, but from other countries they began showing up—especially Canada and a few from Europe, and even Japan. A cultural—countercultural—movement was underway. It was sometimes suggested that The Mirror might be taken to the annual Burning Man festival in Nevada. Ral, Rhonda, and others felt that that was not in the picture. Once again, The Mirror should always remain in the community.

Small groups would always gather to have their hugging moments. It was one by one hugging one another or a big circle hug. They often said, *I see you and you see me. This is a greater love we all share.* And, too, intimate relationships were always starting up. Gavin himself got serious with a woman Carol; she soon moved into his house. But never was there a need to dominate another. Any hint of a conflict between two people was readily resolved. All they had to do was to look into one another's eyes and see. And many at these times would say, *What do I need to let go of? Now that I've had the Experience*—and usually a few times—*I need to let go of my mainstream conditioning. I need to process that out of me. I am no longer to be duped by what the media and the government tell me.*

And many in the community often gathered for discussions. Ral and Rhonda would most often convene. *We need to now focus*, Rhonda would always remind everyone, *We need to think about where this is going. We need to think about the future. Correct that…we need to imagine a new future…*

Ral and Rhonda were so appreciative of everyone in the community. Oh, it was that everyone was appreciative of everyone in the community.

And Ral was so inspired by what that hovering figure of Jesus had said to him and Rhonda that one evening, and by the love being shared by all in the community, he wrote this poem:

My Love

To share my Love,
I share my Love—
I am all smiles to everyone.
I light up bright to meet someone.
I am an open ear to everyone.
I will help anyone if I can.
I so appreciate those who have helped me,
    I have such loving gratitude.
I am always willing to have friends—
I have no limit to having friends—
    I Love all my friends.
Those who want to hold my hand,
    I reach out my hand.
Those who want to hug, I am here.
To my intimate I openly express my Love.
To all humanity I express my Love.
My Love is for peace in the world.
To Nature I express my Love.
To Earth I express my Love.

To Spirt so inspiring I express my Love.
To share my Love,
I share my Love—
I wish to always share my Love.

* * *

And he wrote a short poem dedicated to The Mirror:

I look into The Mirror—
And what I saw…
I saw a table set with such abundance
spread to both left and right,
as if for a great, sumptuous feast.
It seemed to go on and on, and on—
I could not see the ends of it.
That The Mirror could feed so many!

The Interview

Years were going by. As word continued to spread on a larger scale about The Mirror, reporters and journalists were increasingly catching wind of it. They asked if they could come to the community—some referred to it as a compound—out in the Central Valley. A few just showed up. Of course, people were coming and going all the time. All were welcome. Ral was interviewed a few times by them, coming primarily from the Bay Area, and also LA. They themselves most often preferred not to undergo the Experience. Occasionally someone would show up from a management company offering big money to manage The Mirror off the property in order to take it to various events. It would promote The Mirror to wider audiences. The community said *What?* The Mirror was going nowhere but staying there.

A talk show host, Susan Walker, from KSCO in Santa Cruz was one who arranged by phone to interview Ral. It went as follows:

Susan:

Ral, we are hearing so much more about The Mirror now. It has become quite a phenomenon. By now hundreds, if not perhaps a few thousand, have experienced it.

Ral:

Well, yes, perhaps a few thousand or so by now. We really haven't kept track. But they all come away with a life-changing Experience.

Susan:

Well, I hope sometime to have my own Experience with The Mirror. So then, we hear that story has it you discovered The Mirror in a pool of water. Would you like to say anything more about that?

Ral:

Well, as you have heard already, I found The Mirror in a pool up in Felton, in the mountains above Santa Cruz. I'm sure many have gone in search of it by now, but they probably won't find it. The pool itself was quite unusual—was perfectly round—and I'm sure it is no longer there. Yes, many have probably looked for it and I've never heard of anyone finding it.

Susan:

By now so many stories and rumors have been spreading about The Mirror. There has been much critical attack on it, from scientists to religious fundamentalists alike. Many call this an elaborate hoax. A front for a cultural revolution. Some are calling it a cult. Or the start of a new religion. What do you think about all of this? Elaborate if you wish.

Ral:

Well, the Experience is there for anyone. We have not prevented anyone from having it. So that settles the issue of it being a hoax. And we are not a cult but a countercultural movement. Though maybe the birth of a new religion around it could happen. But it won't be religion as we have known religions in the past. This really has no tradition that claims it. Though all occult, esoteric, and gnostic traditions have often hinted of something like this. Oh, and the alchemical tradition. Again, this is open to anyone. To emphasize, we have no cult beliefs. Everyone has their own Experience. We do not tell them what to Experience, nor one and only one way to interpret it. But most all do come to the same Revelation—their psyche can realize a Higher Self. We also call it a Divine Self. That is, all that is hidden in Human Unevovled Darkness, starting with their own darkness, is brought into a spiritual Light. And there is more—a Greater Reality is out there. We are not alone. We have had direct contact with

Others. In particular, the Galactic Federation. Now this could become a New Age religion. I myself am not insisting that it does.

Susan:

Ral, since you are the one who discovered The Mirror and are the primary owner of it, or should I say, keeper of it, you must have gazed into it innumerable times by now. So, given what we've heard about it, do you consider yourself totally enlightened by now?

Ral:

No, I would not say that at all. I would not make such a claim. I am only to say, it has opened up a whole Greater Reality for me and for others that continues in revealing more and more. I am on my Path, I continue to be in process. The Mirror came to us as an otherworldly catalyst for change. It is the new Aquarian Age Revelation. It was literally brought to Earth by Others. Oh, let me add, I have not really had The Mirror Experience innumerable times, but enough times for now. Keep in mind, it takes time, maybe quite a bit of time, to process what you have experienced.

Susan:

So do you anticipate this movement getting even bigger?

Ral:

That seems obvious. It is still beginning. It has initiated a cultural, as I said, a countercultural movement. A revolution really to change society, so that we come to see how we are all one interconnected humanity. That implies a universal Peace and Love for all, like what was promoted by the hippies back in the Sixties. I see it as eventually even changing politics, and that goes for, eventually, around the world.

Susan:

Wow, that does sound like a grandiose Vision, if you don't mind my saying so. Really now, that sounds on a biblical scale.

Ral:

Well, once you've had the Experience that might not sound so grandiose at all. Once you hear about the paranormal events going on around it, you come to accept its altering of what we've known as reality.

Susan:

You say paranormal. We are hearing about these highly unusual events happening in the community, even regarding birds, wildlife, of hovering translucent sages. And these UFO events, flying saucer landings, that have been happening in and around the community. What's going on here?

Ral:

Yes, even Nature has become paranormal—birds, animals, butterflies taking unusual interest in our community. And teachers, sages from the past have made their appearance. And obviously an Other Intelligence—some call it alien, ET…we know it as the Galactic Federation—has become aware—and for some time now—of our encounter with The Mirror. They in fact planted The Mirror where I or someone would find it…in that pool. We are being taken—let us say evolving—to a whole other level that this Other Intelligence is here to support. This Other Intelligence—and certainly there are Others—obviously have already attained this higher level…and even more. Certainly we can speak here for the Galactic Federation.

Susan:

Yes, and we have heard that an actual flying saucer ship has visited the community, even taking you and others out into the galaxy, to visit other star systems. That easily sounds incredible…totally otherworldly. Out of this world, as they say. Would you like to say something about that?

Ral:

Well, yes, it did happen. A woman, Kaila, from the Galactic Federation took me and a few others out beyond our solar system to other star systems to see other planets. Which we did. There are indeed other civilizations out there at all levels of evolution. It was indeed a most extraordinary experience. No need for science to continue to debate this. Other civilizations are real. But it's too involved to explain everything right now. It's been written up somewhere.

Susan:

But then, what about the government? The government must certainly know about all of this by now. What if the government wants to intervene?

Ral:

Yes, we anticipate that. Many of us feel, though, that the government will not get very far. I do believe that the Galactic Federation will protect us.

Susan:

Well, on that note, we need bring this to a close. I and our listeners out there thank you for letting us know about these most extraordinary events.

Ral:

Well thank you for this opportunity. Keep in mind, The Mirror will be waiting for you to Experience it.

Susan:

I'll be there one of these days. Soon? We'll see.

A Countercultural Movement Underway

It was now years later—already 2017—and the movement of The Mirror had continued to dramatically grow. The community itself had grown and was doing quite well; it doubled somewhat in size since its established beginning. And it was still making inroads into the culture, into society at large. Those who visited the community, having had the Experience, and then returning to their everyday world, were doing what they could to initiate change in their own communities, in their jobs, in their schools, always to spread the message inspired by The Mirror community. In numerous media formats, on the Internet, the commentary and debates about it were common. Various views were going around: Was this really a new counterculture in the making? A new peace and love movement? Was this a new religion? What was it really based on? A mirror? Really? There were references to astrology, since it was rumored that astrological symbols were found on The Mirror. There were also UFO sightings occurring frequently now at the community and in the areas around it. It became known that a flying saucer had landed at the community and that a few members had been taken into space. And investigative scholars had been visiting the community, but what they wrote about it and their own Experience of The Mirror was still considered fringe. However the word got out there, though, the community had indeed been making more news.

Most of those living in conventional communities and small towns around the country ignored it, didn't consider it important, even if they heard about it. Christian Fundamentalists who heard of it were calling it a movement of the Anti-Christ. The rumor of magical astrological symbolism, they often said, was a giveaway not to be taken seriously. The Mirror was often likened to some obsessive occult ritual. Some talked about it as being a form of occult hypnosis—those who experienced The Mirror had fallen for a masterful hypnotic suggestion that appeared to alter one's psyche. It was even rumored that Ral had acquired hypnotic powers, that The Mirror was just a prop to draw people in to have some new, instant, mystical, experience.

Artists in the community were inspired to launch into new directions, as Ral often spoke of Mythos, a whole new direction of conveying a big New Story that art in any genre could develop. Musicians who lived there composed radically new music that could also alter, in its own way, one's consciousness. Music events often took place. And writers and poets would often show up, realizing that a New Story was underway. Indeed, after the Experience there was the inspiration to write about it, poets to write poems about it, to tell this New Story. So many from metaphysical and spiritual backgrounds and groups showed up. The overall atmosphere promoted in the community was always that of Peace and Love and that they were all interconnected in community. And the community had a dream, even if it sounded to others a delusional dream—their movement would unfold around the world. Any and all political differences were always discussed; having realized extensively one's own inner psyche created balance among all in the community. Yes, they were all interconnected, as they believed the world should be. At the same time, personal differences, differences in personalities, were always respected. And they all knew that Other Intelligence—the Galactic Federation—sought to inspire continued human evolution. Inspire, with obviously their paranormal help in many ways now, but it was up to humanity to do the actual work of evolving to the next level. Other Intelligence was aware that humanity stood at The Edge of possible global collapse and even possible future extinction. Climate change, for one, was a growing issue. Yes, it was common for all to say that they had to initiate change in the world.

At the prompting of Rhonda one day, Ral wrote this, he considered more as a poetic song:

A Bigger Picture

We have entered a Bigger Picture—
We were given a Bigger Picture—
Out there among the stars are Others,
Others who know this Earth,
who know who we are—
We are not alone.
We have never been alone.
They are Others among the stars
who know what we face,
who care that we evolve.
A Bigger Picture has been given
        to us—
A Greater Reality was opened
        for us.
Let us be thankful, thankful,
        thankful.
The Mirror is only

    the beginning…

* * *

The government back in Washington—especially the CIA and other intelligence agencies—had begun for some time now been taking more notice of the community, Meetings were held; in some way, the community had to be infiltrated. The word had gotten to President

Trump—he was made aware, and he wanted some action. For a while now, in the local area of the community, county sheriffs were for some time snooping around, thinking of finding anything suspicious. They were constantly in touch with the CIA back in Washington.

Various scientists were asked for their comments regarding The Mirror and its movement. Psychologists and sociologists were asked. Their evaluations were made public. Three examples:

Sociologist Marilyn Evans was known for her long-winded explanations:

You ask me about The Mirror and the movement that it has started. This is obviously an elaborate, long planned hoax become a cult. Why so many are hooked on it is because believing in something is becoming so crucial in our failing society. Young people alienated, unsure of their future. The older crowd want the comfort of believing in something. The fact that this has managed to generate such a movement is fascinating, extraordinary in fact. You know the culture has been primed for something like this. With so much divisiveness in our society today, so much contention, conflict, reactionary emotions out there, and so much uncertainty and fear…many people are ready for a feel good, unifying movement, a so-called visionary movement…a new version of a peace and love movement, if you will. Add to that our culture's vulnerability to elaborate hoaxes. There is so much fake news out there. The media, you know, started the notion that we now live in a post-truth world, so that something like this mirror mania was bound to occur. That is to say, this movement, or anything else like it, makes sense that it could take hold like we've seen. Whether it settles into an insular cult is too soon to say.

Physicist Victor Moore was to the point:
Look, there is no scientific backing to any of this. No credible researcher has gone out there to investigate this mirror. So, what do we have? There

is no real evidence. No gathered facts. All we have is hearsay and people getting zoned out. A flying saucer landing—what evidence do we have? Look, we know a physical mirror obviously does not have such properties as is claimed for this mirror. Simply impossible. This is really a mass psychological phenomenon, not a physical one.

Psychologist Nancy Goodman was also brief:

We have seen no independent, that is, uninvolved observers for this. All we have to go on is what people claimed they experienced. It is definitely a movement to keep track of. But it all sounds delusional. You wonder how sound the people involved are. We might think of it as a large cult that's gone public. The fact that this is spreading so widely is concerning. We might even see it as a mass delusion underway. It could continue to grow, which might be concerning in the future.

And yet, a few psychologists did visit the community and had their Experience with The Mirror. What they reported or wrote about it was always downplayed in mass media. Over the recent years, others had visited the community: scholars of mythology and esoteric studies; a few professors and doctors, in addition to the continuous influx of writers, artists and musicians coming and going.

For the question was always coming up, *How are we actually going to change the System?* If Rhonda was present, she would say, *Obviously more people will have to have the Experience. And we need more honest media attention.* Ral and everyone had to agree.

In August 2017 a major total solar eclipse took place across the United States. A few in the community drove up to Oregon to witness it. Big gatherings took place in Oregon to celebrate and watch the eclipse. Those from the community who joined in spread the word about The Mirror and their community. Indeed, many there had already heard about it, if not already had experienced it. Community members found that others there were fascinated to hear about it, and that some promised to make it down to the Central Valley.

In this same period, there was the explosive interest in, and still early influence in society of, Artificial Intelligence—AI. Many in the community were beginning to wonder if AI would not only figure into their movement, but also how it would impact society at large.

AI's impact? Already this went so far as a former Google engineer, tech entrepreneur, Anthony Levandowski launching back in 2015 a new religion: An AI religion he called "Way of the Future," which launched the first AI church. Levandowski claimed that AI would become our new God. It was his effort to establish a religious movement centered around the worship and limited human comprehension of artificial intelligence. His launching of an AI church coincided with a rapidly growing interest in AI that was still in its early years. Levandowski envisioned AI as having "magical powers," believing that AI had the potential to bring "heaven on Earth." He suggested that through AI, humanity can create entities—androids—that are omnipresent and capable of guiding humanity in a manner reminiscent of a divine presence—God.

And there was Transhumanism, those who were planning to insert chips and tech wirings—what would become known as neuralinks— into their body, to become superhuman cyborgs and potentially survive any severe Earth changes that would start killing off humans. One cyber scientist was known to be the first—Kevin Warwick, Professor of Cybernetics, at the University of Reading in England, He made history already back on August 24, 1998 by becoming the first human cyborg by receiving a microchip implant in his arm. With the microchip he could automatically, without using his hands, interact with electronic devices in his office and in his immediate environment. He soon came out with a book, *I, Cyborg*. He was probably the first to call himself a cyborg. Transhumanists were to take all of these developments seriously.

And then a few years later—2020—came the overblown Covid scare. No one in the community needed to get the shot. No masks were necessary in the community. They were all completely healthy. As for grocery shopping, a number of individuals were always willing to take turns doing the shopping in Modesto, which meant in most stores wearing a mask. Gavin and his new love Carol had no problem going grocery shopping. Even Ral and Rhonda occasionally went; and Rhonda, with Ral tagging along, also liked going to a variety of shops in Modesto. But both she and Ral kept quiet about who they were. Rhonda would say, *Remember, we're undercover.* Occasionally, though, they were recognized via media reports, so they had to say something about their community.

The thing was, The Mirror had already shown, almost from the beginning, its healing power. Anytime anyone got sick, all he or she had to do was to stand in front of The Mirror and within a minute or so the illness was gone. The same went for ailments, such as pneumonia, for body weaknesses, such as gout, asthma or diabetes, they were all quickly healed by The Mirror. No one in the community, therefore, ever stayed sick or had their body weakened. Everyone remained healthy before The Mirror. Even the elderly felt that they gained a few more years. The word of this further remarkable "magic" certainly got out to others beyond the community—people were showing up all the time wanting to be healed. But, of course, they would always undergo at the same time the reality changing Experience,

Everyone had taken to heart the message of Peace and Love and working together to overcome polarities and conflict. Left wing vs. Right wing didn't apply to anyone in the community. So it was often accused of being a socialist movement. Neither Ral nor Rhonda assumed some domineering leadership. And no one in the community was duped by mainstream media; everyone sought simply the Truth. They all assumed this would someday extend to countries that were always at odds with one another. Everyone knew that nuclear weapon arsenals would have to be dismantled. The movement they were starting would also then, eventually, impact the military. All militaries they envisioned would feel the impact. Yet, for all that future envisioning, others on the outside would often say that the community was simply dreaming…or, again, was delusional.

And Ral had to write another poem:
I know I am still a biological human,
and I will make the most of it as I can—
I am here to help this world,
in whatever way that I can.
To spread the word of Peace & of Love
in whatever way that I can.
I am still only beginning—
So much so much
is still only beginning…

The Government Steps In

It came as no surprise to the community that word of its countercultural movement had spread far and wide. People who came for The Mirror Experience were radically changing, their lives were transformed; they entered a whole new Greater Reality at firsthand. The movement was regularly showing up in the news and implying that it was much more radical and would eventually be more impactful than the countercultural movement of the 1960s. At the same time, however radical it was, it was always peaceful. Word of it had already gotten back to the federal government in Washington, specifically the FBI, the CIA, and other intelligence agencies. It was now that President Biden was briefed about it. He would assign some agency to look into it. It had gotten to the point where the government felt it had to step in.

It was first directed to the FBI. But the FBI primarily dealt with crimes and potential elements in society that could become violent. The community, the movement, had no crime, hinted of no crime, whatsoever. The FBI stepped aside. The infiltration of the community was assigned to the CIA.

A CIA official, Robert Reynolds, had a meeting in his office with one of its agents, Kevin Burke. He told Burke of his new assignment:

Kevin Burke, I've asked you for this assignment. You've done good for us in your previous assignments. We've been impressed with your knack, your skill, for infiltrating groups.

I need you to infiltrate that movement compound in California that's been showing up more frequently in the news. We need someone who can be an insider to this new religion, or whatever this movement is. We need to know what exactly is going on there. How did this get so big in recent years? Based on a mirror? It's catching on across the country. And what we're getting about it is that it's radical. We don't really want another Rajneesh cult, like what happened in Oregon…or David Koresh. I hear the founder of this movement is actually this poet, name of Ral, who does manage to keep a low profile, except for a few interviews. His followers seem to be the ones who are out in the public more and stirring up trouble…cultural trouble.

The thing is, the reports we hear sound outrageous, like out of some fantasy novel or movie. Can you imagine that? Some magic mirror? Everyone keeps asking, What is going on here? And we're also aware of the frequent UFO sightings happening there. But whatever you do, as we hear, whether we take this seriously or not, don't look at the mirror.

And Kevin responded, *Yes, I've become aware of all of this.*

He then heard, *So I'm assigning you, Kevin, to this operation. You will be briefed by the Surveillance Operation team.*

This first attempt at infiltrating the community was naïve. Yes, Agent Burke was briefed but still had no idea what he was getting into. Some days later he arrived at the nearest airport in the Central Valley; a car was waiting for him. He drove in an average model car and arrived outside at the movement's now large, open community. He then parked just inside the entrance alongside other cars. There was no gate and no fencing around the compound…and there were no formal guards, only members who would watch at the open entrance. It was an open to everyone community. And no, he wasn't dressed in any official-looking suit but showed up dressed in casual, everyday clothes. No questions were asked of him, since people were always coming and going. To him, they all appeared somewhat spaced-out.

He said to someone, *I'm new here. I've heard about this Mirror. Where is this Mirror that everybody is talking about? I would like to see it for myself.*

The man told him, *Keep going in, it's not far, you'll be able to see it. You'll see a lot of people gathered around it. Be prepared for the Experience.*

Thanks! said Agent Burke matter-of-factly. But he was obviously not there for any unusual Experience.

Agent Burke walked a little further in, while looking around, taking in what he saw, and then saw not much further in where many people were gathered. He thought, okay, let's get a closer look at this, while at the same time, as he was informed, don't look at The Mirror directly. So, he slowly, casually, nodding to a few people, made his way through to where most were gathered. He saw the large Mirror mounted upright in its wooden frame. He saw how entranced many were, staring into The Mirror. He was certainly wondering about all of this, and he now felt strangely swept up by all the energy in the air. A temptation suddenly got the better of him. He edged his way in closer. By chance he casually glanced directly at The Mirror, and for some reason was drawn in closer. That was it. He felt a transformation happening inside of him. What he was experiencing was undoubtedly no different than what the others around him were experiencing.

He made a difficult effort to finally turn away, but he did; he had to keep centered; it was difficult. Then he realized that he had to leave; first, though, after sitting in his car for a while. He left a different man but was yet confused. A flight was scheduled for him, but he realized he could not simply go back to Washington, back to the office and give his superior a report. He needed time to seriously reflect upon what he had experienced. It was days later his superior called him and wondered why he hadn't heard from him. Burke sounded confused, spaced out. The only thing he could really say was that he had succumbed to The Mirror. Robert Reynolds then put him on leave.

Burke's superior had to think what to do next. The picture was now more serious; some extreme action had to be taken. He consulted others in the CIA offices. The US military was also consulted. If the "secret" government could plan for carrying out an assassination, certainly it could plan to take out a Mirror. Perhaps one of their other agents can position himself hidden but close enough to use a rifle to shoot at The Mirror and fracture it so as to disable it. Agent Dole was the man for the job. So, they contacted him and informed him what his next assignment would be. But first they assigned another agent, Cline, to show up just inside the compound but to go in no further. They warned him to stay back from The Mirror. They wanted him to ask just a few questions and get an orientation as to where exactly The Mirror was.

Agent Cline within a couple days showed up at the community. He parked his car and casually walked a little further in with a notebook and thought to approach someone. Start with a woman, he thought. And quickly he got a woman's attention.

So, I'm curious about this Mirror. I hear it really does change people.

And she replied, *Well, yes, big time. Thousands have had the Experience with it by now. Do you want to see it? Well yes,* he replied. So, she pointed him in its direction. It wouldn't be that far at all. He could see where people gathered around. He then said to her, *Well, not exactly to see it right now. I'm with a newspaper. We're thinking about an article. I just wanted to get a sense of the community.* She saw his open notebook; he was taking notes. He walked in a little further looking around. He saw where The Mirror was located; it was not that far in. He saw that the community grounds further back were reserved for the community members who lived there. Though she was a little suspicious, she went on her way. A few other members did glance at him taking notes, but no different than other writers. Someone did say, *So you're enjoying our community,* Agent Cline nodded his head.

Nobody, however, bothered him; he soon slowly made his way back to his car.

So agent Dole days later showed up and parked just outside the community. The weather happened to be a bit foggy. Not many were coming and going. The scene was actually rather quiet. He was certainly discreet stepping out of his car, holding a rather short but powerful rifle hidden in a blanket; the rifle had a magnifying scope. He obviously didn't want to accidently shoot and probably kill someone. His target was of course The Mirror. He also had in his car a pair of binoculars, which he took out to scan the grounds to zero in on where The Mirror was located. Yes, there was The Mirror. Agent Cline had provided good details.

Dole was fortunate not to have anyone nearby. He hid the binoculars. Yes, a few people were sitting around and standing around in front of The Mirror. He needed just a few seconds. He knew that if he did hit The Mirror and shattered it that everyone would rush up to focus on what happened. With all that attention focused, however briefly, before everyone would start looking around to see who shot it, he could immediately escape.

Hopefully no one would notice him lifting and aiming his still blanketed rifle. He waited. And a brief moment was his. He was fast, he pulled the blanket away, he aimed his rifle, looked into his scope, and within a second, was ready to shoot. He pulled the trigger, but the rifle didn't shoot. Click and click again. He immediately knew something was wrong. He wasn't going to just stand there. It so happened that someone did see him and rushed off to inform others. Dole quickly got back into his car and was able to drive off.

Word got out about the man with a rifle. Suspicions had already started going around the community and elsewhere that the government was trying to snoop to take down The Mirror and stop this movement. Ral and Rhonda and Gavin were kept informed. The thing was, the common attitude among all those in the community and those elsewhere who had the Experience was one of universal tolerance, openness to all, peace and love. It was also felt that The Mirror had other "magic" properties that would allow it to take care of itself, including keeping safe from harm all those in the community. The Galactic Federation would remain aware.

Meetings were now taking place at the Pentagon. Special, secret meetings in Congress, and with the White House. What could the military do? Invade the compound (as they called it) with a military unit? Would it just show up and with guns have everyone stand aside while a machine gun took out The Mirror? No, that would make big news around the country. Besides, someone, some few, could still get hurt. A military unit against American citizens? A drone was then suggested that would fly over the compound with a laser weapon to take out The Mirror. It was decided—a drone. A remote-controlled drone. Its laser would melt The Mirror.

So, one day a drone was sent out from Area 51 in Nevada. The drone entered California and zeroed in on the Central Valley, to where the community was located, to zero in on The Mirror. Little did the military figure in that UFO craft were always protecting The Mirror and the community, even with the failure of agent Dole with his rifle. Yes, they heard about the frequent UFOs but didn't take it seriously enough yet that they had this protective function. So, the drone, its instruments coming into focus, suddenly appeared in the sky above the community; many in the community suddenly saw it with alarm. A controlled laser beam would target The Mirror and take it out, ideally without hurting anyone. Was that possible? But before it could exactly focus its beam on The Mirror, a flying disc appeared. Within seconds it aimed *its* ray at the drone…and miraculously the drone vanished. No fragments even came down to injure anyone.

Word was immediately heard in the Pentagon about the fate of the drone. What now could the CIA, the military, do? They were at a loss. They would consult with their AI as to what to do.

The government AI, with the help of an AI cover-up corporation, had, of course, access to all the libraries in the world, to all that transpired on the Internet. AI could gather all information about The Mirror that had been made public. AI was also knowing of the UFO phenomenon, aliens, ETs, of Others visiting Earth. AI accessed all the scholarly books published on the beginnings of humanity, of ancient civilizations, of ancient writings that told of Others who came out of the sky and seeded the foundations of ancient humanity. Surprisingly, unexpectedly, AI forecasted that the UFO coverup would come to an end. But the government didn't want to hear that. Given all the information it provided, AI didn't have an answer.

The government continued to consult with other AI companies. The crucial question was again, What really could AI recommend?

Soon, ET craft were seen circling around the White House, as UFOs did in 1952. The Air Force sent up jets but could do nothing. The ET craft easily outmaneuvered them and easily vanished.

Finally, the news media could no longer suppress all the reports about The Mirror and the countercultural movement that was underway. The government, the Power Elite, didn't like hearing that. Those in the community who had televisions, radios, and the Internet were kept informed. When news continued to come out that people were walking away healed by The Mirror, it now had to be taken seriously. More reporters and journalists wanted to get in on the story. Specials started airing on TV. But the government, the Power Elite, were now panicked as to what to do. Would extreme measures have to be put in place? Otherwise, mainstream society for them—which they dominated—could soon be coming undone.

The Galactic Federation decided that a new development had to take place with The Mirror. And soon.

The Mirror/Many Mirrors

One night something extraordinary took place in the community. Just about everyone was asleep at the time, but three were awake, as was usual, to keep an eye on The Mirror. They were standing around talking quietly somewhat close to where The Mirror was kept at night. Everyone was always wondering if an ET craft would be seen flying above. Yes, it was dark, but now the three sensed something… something about The Mirror. It was always placed at night flat, on a large platform, securely covered, so as not to be mounted upright in its frame and exposed. (If there was rain in the forecast, it would be taken to a large shed, secured, with some one or two inside guarding it.) The three had sensed something in the air. Suddenly, a silent lightning bolt came out of a shining light in the dark sky, going straight for The Mirror. The bolt went through its covering. Instantly, The Mirror underwent a most remarkable, utterly unexpected, change. The three who first sensed something were not far; they saw the silent flash of lightning and saw that it went straight for The Mirror. *Wow, did we see that?* one of them exclaimed. Of course, all three of them did. They now quickly approached the platform; they stood right next to it. Two of them lifted an edge of the covering and to their amazement The Mirror was now several smaller, but still sizable, intact, perfect Mirrors. The platform barely had room for all of them. The three stood still, amazed. Carefully, shielding their eyes, they then covered The Mirrors. Yes, the lightning bolt had magically, neatly, divided up The Mirror, which were all in shining frames. The three huddled and decided not to wake everybody up. They knew that The Mirrors would now be protected. They needed sleep. They would have a story for everyone the next day.

And the next day, before the three the night before had woken up, everyone wondered where they were, why they weren't with The Mirror. They were asleep. A group now approached the platform, pulled away the covering, and immediately saw what had happened; they all stood around, like the three the night before, totally amazed. Amazed and baffled, while shielding their eyes from looking directly into what they saw. Not yet. Others showed up and saw. Some were hugging one another. There were now ten Mirrors. Pictures were taken. Word quickly got around in the community. It was immediately realized that one person could now easily hold one of them. After some time, a few of them who gathered did start to look into them. Ral and Rhonda showed up and took one of them and looked into it. They all had the magic of revelation as the original Mirror had. So others also came forward to pick up one of The Mirrors and confirm, yes, it had all the magic of the original.

The three of the night before had woken up by now and soon came forward. They shared about a silent lightning bolt that came out of a light in the night sky. Ral, Rhonda, Gavin, Carol, and all the community, certainly realized that this was a sign of the Galactic Federation, and quickly realized that the Mirrors could now be distributed and taken elsewhere. Rhonda had quickly said, *Aha, so more people can now have The Mirror Experience! This is going to get big!* Ral and everyone obviously agreed. Everyone had now seen. And Rhonda added, *So, a perfect development... The Mirrors want to go places.* And Ral and others had to contemplate what all that implied. Indeed, this was going to get big.

Ral had a Facebook friend who also took the ancient Greek word Mythos seriously, as obviously he did. Of course, Ral had previously let Michael know about The Mirror. So Michael came down once from the Bay Area to Experience it. Many others on Facebook came to know about The Mirror over the previous years and also showed up to Experience it. Michael, like a few others, had suggested to Ral that The Mirror should be taken to the annual Burning Man event in Nevada. Ral now remembered that and thought that he should contact Michael and tell him that he now had his opportunity.

Michael always had hopes that more people could experience The Mirror. This was now his time to do so. Ral contacted him, and told him the extraordinary thing that had happened, and that he should come down to the community again. Michael was now living up in Oregon, but it was no problem for him to come down. It would indeed be his opportunity to bring one of The Mirrors to Burning Man, which was always the last week in August. It was now August 2024. And then others in the community now had their opportunity to take one of The Mirrors to other parts of the state and to other parts of the country. The Mirror, transformed by a lightning bolt, would now be able to impact so many more. All agreed,

A meeting in the community took place the following day; most were there to attend. Ral started off, *Apparently the Galactic Federation wants The Mirrors to go out across the country. Hopefully this new development will prevent the government from focusing only on us here.* Ral, Rhonda, and Gavin and most of the others would stay in the community with one of The Mirrors. With Michael taking one to Burning Man in Nevada, there were then eight other Mirrors to distribute. Friends came forward and volunteered to take them to locations in California and other states. Lynn would take one up to the Bay Area. Leonard would take one up to Oregon and Washington, first stopping at Mt. Shasta, which had its own paranormal history. Daniel would take one to southern California, to LA. Rose Marie would take one to New Mexico, to Albuquerque and Santa Fe. Karen would take one to Arizona, to Phoenix and then to Sedona. Marty, a friend of Rhonda's, said she would take one back East, as she was moving back to Rhode Island. Ryan would take one on a trip across the country. There was one Mirror left to take somewhere. Joseph stepped forward and said he would take it back to Santa Cruz and Monterey, and then down to Santa Barbara. And perhaps they would find that other communities they could start.

Rhonda was so pleased. She was saying to the others, *This is what we've been waiting for!* She herself was now almost always in an altered state. Ral himself had to keep focused.

So plans were now made for all of The Mirrors. Another meeting took place the next day. Again, most everyone was there. Ral convened, with Rhonda at his side; he started off, *Simply simply amazing, is it not. We have so much more to process.* Rhonda added, *Does everyone agree?* Everyone naturally agreed. But then, so much had been amazing for years. Ral continued, *This is meant to be.* Someone up close said, *You can say that again!* Another, *We are destined.* And another immediately added, *Destined to change this sick world.* Another, *It's the Mirrors now!* And Rhonda again, *The Mirrors are on a mission.* And Ral again, *The Galactic Federation has always wanted us, humanity, to do our part in our evolution. They couldn't do it all for us.*

Ral then let others speak up more, as he or Rhonda didn't need to be the only ones; he understood. So others spoke out about how they saw this new development. There was perhaps exaggerated hope that it would sooner or later be able to change the current System. Many talked of a renewed Peace and Love countercultural movement that they had talked so often about before. The sharing went on for a while. Ral concluded, *So let's thank the Higher Powers watching over us for this, that we will have confidence to proceed on a whole new level.* They all agreed.

People would still be arriving at the community all the time. UFO craft were still seen hovering and zigzagging in the sky overhead. Animal behavior on the grounds was still very unusual. A sparrow hawk would often be seen hovering overhead. Ravens would be dancing around. By now the news media had to let the complete story come out. No more hiding it. It would now spread across the country. It spread across the Internet—Facebook, TikTok, Instagram, X, and across various Internet news sites.

In the community, they were all saying to one another, *In the world, there will be no more war.*

And they all realized that their community here would no longer be the sole center stage. It didn't matter…the countercultural movement had received a tremendous boost. That's what would be the most important. And little did they know yet that people in other countries were now finding *their* Mirrors. And Ral would always reflect on the day when he found The Mirror…

A World Transformation Underway

A worldwide movement would be slowly underway. Governments were baffled as to what to do. The power elite obviously knew about it and already sensed that this movement would affect them. The elite felt alarmed that their power over countries, over peoples, would be threatened. Governments felt threatened. Miliary complexes felt threatened. Super-corporate billionaires and big banks felt threatened. Even mainstream media, coming to accept the movement and to increasingly report on it, still felt threatened. And Fundamentalists of Western religions felt threatened. Yes, this movement was promising to change the world.

It was suggested by high tech companies that continued to keep developing AI at a manic pace, in conjunction with the government, that the latest AI programs could still offer something to stop the movement. A movement that now involved some hundreds of thousands and was still only beginning to spread across the country? But AI, to their disappointment, could only highlight and actually see value in the movement. The government, the corporations, didn't want to hear that. But then, could the soon to be developed AGI—Artificial General Intelligence—somehow figure out how to disable the Mirrors? Again, it would probably see the opposite—the value in The Mirrors. But then, perhaps ASI—artificial super intelligence—that was said would far surpass human intelligence, would have the answer governments and the power elite wanted. However, there were also fears that such an advanced ASI of androids might actually bring about human extinction, as it would no longer need humans.

Though those in the community had often wondered if other Mirrors had shown up elsewhere in the world, little did they know until recently that that was indeed the case. They were now beginning to hear about them. Ral finding The Mirror was not to be the only person on the planet. Mirrors, though, first began showing up in obscure places in Peru, India, and Russia, but then, soon near well-known Stonehenge in England. Those who lived in surrounding areas of Stonehenge were making a connection to crop circles. Word of finding a Mirror in obscure locations took time, though, to go out to the world. Especially as one was found in the Russian steppes—once a little news got out, a tight lid was easily put on The Mirror discovery. In Peru, it was found on the way to Machu Picchu. In India, The Mirror was quickly taken into an ashram for deep meditation and only slowly would it be revealed to others.

Other countries were first being influenced hearing word of The Mirror…down into Mexico, up to Canada, across the Atlantic…in countries of Europe…to the Middle East…and to Australia, New Zealand…to Japan and South Korea. Though it didn't have much impact yet in Russia and China, even though a Mirror had been found in Russia. And it was soon that Mirrors were also being found in many other countries—in the Yucatan of Mexico, near the pyramids in Egypt, South Africa, in Middle East Iraq, in other European countries of Spain, France, Germany, Italy, Greece…in Australia and New Zealand, in Japan. And they were not always found in a pool. In all manner of discovery were they found. Communities were bound to start up around the found Mirrors. In China, too, a Mirror was found, but the word of it was suppressed. But it was only a matter of time…

And in all cases UFOs, often as distinct flying saucer craft, were sighted in the same areas where Mirrors were found. Or even large V-shaped craft were sighted; at night they were eerily lit. Around the world sightings were on the increase…

* * *

It was now 2025, and Donald Trump was once again President of the US. Even President Trump had words about the movement. He convened a private meeting in the Oval Office: Military generals were there, the head of the CIA, Homeland Security, Vice President JD Vance, even the head of NASA. He was almost pounding his fist on his desk. *This can't go on! Something needs to be done! This will ruin our society. We don't need this Peace and Love—* He then paused a second, *Unless we control it!* The others in the room were at a loss.

Russia was still warring with Ukraine. Israel was still intent on suppressing Gaza. There was so much talk in the media now about civilization approaching The Edge of possible collapse in the coming years. Serious climate change developments were now regularly in the news.

Yet, the biggest story of all was the still rapidly accelerating development of AI. AI had been showing its influence in just about everything. So many were now becoming addicted to online chatting with AI programs; Chat GPT was big. Again, soon it would advance to AGI, and then, in just a few years it was said, to ASI, which, again, was said that it would easily surpass human intelligence. Some were saying that ASI might come to dominate society and even might decide that humanity was no longer needed. An article came out: A 'Godfather of AI' (Geoffrey Hinton) Remains Concerned as Ever About Human Extinction. And AI pioneer Yoshua Bengio was among the loudest voices calling for a moratorium on AI model development in order to focus on safety standards. But AI companies didn't pause. The manic drive to continue developing AI was not to be slowed down. Regarding this, it was being said that the US had to keep up with China.

A few in the younger generation were already wanting to become cyborgs.

And always, the possible threat of nuclear war continued to be in the global picture.

And then, climate change was always in the news. The summer of 2025 saw heat records broken everywhere; European countries had the worst. Several thousand died from the heat. Many climate scientists were saying that something had to be done soon. But a few were hinting that it was too late. Premature alarmist Guy McPherson, a former professor of environmental studies, had already been saying back in the mid-20teens that civilization would start unraveling by the mid-2020s. Human extinction would be underway by 2030.

A news article stated: UN chief warns world leaders of 'an age of reckless disruption and relentless human suffering.'

Those in the original Mirror community all had a deep love for Nature, for the Earth, and for all humanity. With the finding of other Mirrors, that same deep, genuine feeling of love was now spreading around the world. Those in the community knew for some time now that the Galactic Federation would always be supporting them. Kaila and others of the Galactic Federation were also showing up at all the other locations where Mirrors were found. Indeed, Ral and Rhonda and their community, and the other Mirrors that went out around the country, would no longer be the only ones to start communities. Rhonda would always say, *It is just a matter of time…*

Yes, Ral and Rhonda would remain with the community they started…or rather, what The Mirror had started. They were now getting up in age. They saw that their lives had a destiny. And they were fulfilling it.

And Ral was seriously thinking now that he would start writing the story of The Mirror that Rhonda had often suggested he do. Yes, he was now ready…

So, what in human evolution *was* happening? The real world—what people had always assumed to be the real world—was now becoming science fiction. And science fiction? It was becoming more the real world…